THE
TREASURE
OF PERIL
ISLAND

C.W. JAMES

INSUNDRY
PRODUCTIONS
BOOKS

Gardnerville, NV
www.InsundryProductions.com

Cover design and interior layout by MiblArt.com

Special Thanks to
Sidney Drew

CHAPTER ONE

"Yo-heave-ho! and they call it piracy...
With the Roger at the truck, yo-ho, my comrades bold,
Yo-heave-ho! there's lots of gold at sea.
A merry life, a short life, a noose for you and me;
And Davy Jones must have our bones,
If they call it piracy."

In the stuffy cabin of the barge, Jack Drayton looked up from his book of Shakespeare sonnets. He was hunched up at the small table, attempting to get the most light on the pages from the cracked lamp; it smoked in the draft, filling the narrow place with an odor of bad petroleum.

He turned his head to listen, irritated at the interruption. He had discovered the forgotten volume behind a bench while walking along the Embankment, and he pounced on it. The only thing he missed about not living at his uncle's house was its library. Buying books was not in his tiny budget nowadays, so he hungered for print.

The hoarse and lusty voices swelled louder and nearer. Then they died away, and were followed by a slight shock and a grating sound as a boat laid up to Jack's ancient barge.

"Steady, you clumsy lubber," said a drawling voice. "Where are you steering?"

"I ain't a cat, Honorable, am I? I can't see in a fog thick enough to cut marlinspikes out of. Hello, it looks as if there was passengers on this floatin' 'otel. Ahoy, messmate!"

Jack did not stir. He didn't want to have his reading disturbed by a party of drunken sailors. Perhaps his unwanted visitors would leave.

"Ahoy, *Etruria*," called a man's voice. "Heave to! We've got dispatches for you from the German Hemperor."

Jack heard a step on the deck. He sighed and leaned back in his chair. No, they weren't going to leave; he had to talk to them. Taking up the lamp, he opened the door. The rain fell dismally, quenching the few sparks that sometimes shot from the chimney of his ancient barge.

A repulsive little ogre, stunted and hideous, leered at him as he stepped from the darkness. He held a clay pipe in his horribly twisted mouth. He removed it, spat upon the deck, and grinned, revealing two long teeth through his mustache. It occurred to Jack that the man bore some strong resemblance to an animal — a weasel.

"What do you want with me?" asked Jack in an uninterested tone.

"Where's Lucknan's wharf, my handsome curly-aired youth?"

"About six hundred yards below on this side." The little man didn't move. "Can I do anything else for you?"

"Got any drink aboard, my noble guide-book?" croaked the caller.

"Nothing except water, I'm afraid."

The uninvited visitor spat again and leered at Jack with his ferret eyes. In the light of the lamp, they almost appeared red.

"It's a good job I believe you, my young lad. If I looked and found you lyin', I'd twist the 'ead off you. Good-night, mate. 'Ere, won't you kiss me good night? He, he, he, he!"

With one light, catlike bound he vanished into the gloom, croaking and cackling like a raven. Jack shook his head and returned to the cabin.

"Is it unhealthy in there, Monkey?" drawled one of the occupants of the boat.

"Smells like a gas-works, Honorable."

"Dear me, how dreadful! I must let in some fresh air."

An oar battered in the cabin's little window.

"The drunken blackguards!" Jack spat out. He regained the deck, but the boat had already pulled away.

Jack swore. Outside, the black waves of the great river Thames surged past his anchored barge. London's faint lights blinked from the farther shore, sirens snorted in the gathering fog, and ghostly vessels flitted seaward with the falling tide. He counted the hollow strokes of a church clock somewhere nearby: eight.

He again went down to the cabin, and felt a pang of hunger. He had been engrossed in the beauty of Shakespeare's language and the joy of reading so much that he had completely lost track of time. He opened a cupboard. It was bare.

"Old Mother Hubbard, went to the cupboard," Jack sighed. He dug into his pocket and brought out his entire earthly wealth.

"One and eightpence-halfpenny," he laughed ruefully.

He stepped over to the tiny closet and opened it. His other suit and shirt hung in it, marginally better than the shabby ones he was currently wearing. Next to it was his steward's uniform, still in good shape. Luckily, he decided not to dispose of it after his last voyage as he had planned.

He couldn't afford to buy a new one now. He had heard that the White Star Line was going to expand service on their North Atlantic runs, so he decided earlier that day, albeit with some reluctance, to visit their office. Signing up again as a ship's steward would be preferable to starvation, but he needed a new collar to be at least presentable.

"Say sevenpence-halfpenny for a collar, and I could eat for a tenpence," he calculated out loud. "That would leave something for tomorrow."

He pocketed his money, pulled on his ancient pea-coat and cap, and went back on deck. The rain had stopped, but he could feel its wet threat. Perhaps he could get to shore before the rain began again. It was then that he discovered his boat was missing. The severed hawser told the tale.

"Those drunken brutes cut it loose!" he growled. "If I can't get ashore, I can't eat ... hello!" He heard oars splashing. "Hello!" he cried out.

"Hello!" came back the answer.

"Going ashore?" shouted Jack.

"Aye, mate."

"Then you might come alongside and give me a passage. My tub has broken adrift."

There was a lamp in the boat. The tide was running out swiftly, but the man in the boat was a clever oarsman and started maneuvering to the barge.

"Hold on," Jack said. "I forgot to tell you I'm broke."

The boat pulled up next to the barge. "That ain't uncommon on the river, mate," said the man in the boat, "sailors can't hang on to guineas, somehow. I don't want paying for punting ye across. I'm pulling for Lucknan's Wharf."

Jack extinguished the lamp, locked the cabin door, and swung himself into the boat. "I'm much obliged to you."

The two sat in silence for a while as Jack stared at the approaching shore.

"Like a teeming city, the river knows no sleep. Day and night glad hearts and sorrowful hearts are rocked on its bosom. Day and night bears back men and women to happy English homes; night and day it separates loved ones from loved ones outward bound for lands of brighter sunshine and more gorgeous flowers, perhaps — but flowers and sunshine cannot make home," Jack softly said.

"Very pretty," the man at the oars said. "Are ye a poet?"

Jack shook his head and grinned. He pulled his pea-coat tighter. "No. I was just reading some."

The man grunted something and continued to ply the oars. They were close to the bank before Jack suddenly remembered that Marsden, a friendly local waterman who extended Jack credit, wouldn't be working again until early tomorrow morning. Jack couldn't, in common decency, ask the stranger to row him all the way back to the barge. That meant spending the night on shore in the rain. It was not a cheerful prospect.

After more silent minutes, they reached the wharf, a dim gas lamp flickering dismally at the far end. As the man made the boat fast, Jack finally had a clear view of him as he raised his head. He might have been sixty, seventy, a hundred. Long hair, white as snow, hung over his shoulders. The long cloak he wore fell open, and Jack drew his breath with a soft hiss.

He caught a glimpse of buckled shoes, knee-breeches, and a coat with wide lappets and laced cuffs. A sword hung at the old man's hip, and two huge, old-fashioned pistols were thrust under his belt. When he lifted a three-cornered hat from the thwart and put it on his head, two little black eyes twinkled at him from under the shaggy eyebrows.

"You're a bold lad or a brainless one," said the oddly dressed man, "and by the build of ye, ye'd serve the King well. I like your figurehead and your spars. There's a slimness about ye that means speed, and still a breadth o' beam that shows ye'd ride out many a gale. Take my advice, lad, and get into harbor, or serve the King ye must, willy-nilly. Set all sail for port afore the press-gangs are on ye, for it's trim vessels like ye are they want."

Press-gangs! In 1903? Jack almost burst out laughing, but covered himself by clambering out of the boat. The Royal Navy ended that practice of taking of men into navy by force back in the early part of the last century. So the old man must be mad. He was one of the few grand old hulks who had out-weathered the gales of time, perhaps, and was living the old days over again when three-decker grappled with three-decker, and chain-shot snapped masts away like carrots.

"Did ye ever go to sea?" the old man asked.

"Yes, for a couple of years," Jack didn't think he needed to add that it was as a mere steward on various passenger liners.

"Ah!" The old man gripped Jack's hand eagerly. "Did ye ever meet Dick Swayne?"

Jack thought it best to humor him, even though the name meant nothing to him.

"No, never," he said.

The old man let go of Jack's hand. "Then ye were in luck. I know him, and he knows me. He's always hunting for me; but I'm too cunning. If ever ye meet Dick Swayne, lad, run him through, and when ye've run him through blow out his brains to make sure he's dead. Then there's the Frenchy, Lake, and the Honorable. Shoot 'em down, lad, shoot 'em down like dogs."

The rain started again.

"You'll be drenched if you stay here," Jack said, trying to change the subject. "It's raining faster than ever."

The old man's jaw dropped, and his sparkling eyes grew stony with horror. He grabbed onto Jack's shoulders, his fingers digging in. "Hark! Did ye ever hear the old song? D'ye hear that? D'ye hear it, lad?"

Faintly through the mist and rain came the distant sound of voices singing the sea-chorus Jack had heard once before that night:

"Yo-heave-ho! and they call it piracy...
With the Roger at the truck, yo-ho, my comrades bold,
Yo-heave-ho! there's lots of gold at sea.
A merry life, a short life, a noose for you and me;
And Davy Jones must have our bones,
If they call it piracy."

The old man staggered, and Jack caught him, thinking he was about to fall.

"It's Dick Swayne and the Frenchy," he gasped. Then he stood erect, as though transformed into a much younger man. His voice lost its mad ring, and took on the tone of command.

"Stand by me, lad, stand by me. I'll take their challenge. Are ye armed? Nay? Here, take that. It's a hair trigger and the flint's new." He called out to the skies. "Have at ye, have at ye, dogs!"

Before Jack could answer, the old man thrust one of the monstrous pistols into Jack's hand and began to run at amazing speed towards the network of dark streets beyond the wharf.

By Heavens, he'll kill somebody! Jack thought. He cupped his free hand to his mouth and shouted. "Come back, come back!" Dreading that the poor lunatic might come to some harm, Jack started in pursuit.

He left the feeble, sputtering light of the gas lamp, and entered into darkness. Black warehouses pressed in on either side; the leaden sky overhead was only slightly less dark. He stopped at an intersection of two narrow streets. He couldn't see his quarry. Then he caught a glimpse of a flashing naked sword, and the old man's cracked voice rang out in wild defiance:

"Yo-heave-ho! there's lots of cold at sea,
Aw merry life, a short life, a noose for you and me –
And Davy Jones must have our bones,
If they call it piracy."

A wolfish yell answered, and heavy boots clattered on the wet cement, on the street off to Jack's left. Four figures rushed out of the shadows.

"Have at ye, dogs, have at ye!" cried the old man.

"Stun him, but be careful," ordered a second voice. "If we kill him the chance is gone."

Jack charged toward the sound of the conflict. He unexpectedly emerged on the fight out of the darkness. The lunatic had his back to the wall, his three attackers around him in a semi-circle, like a pack of wolves closing in on a deer. As one of the three made a move in, the old man lunged at them with his sword as he hissed out a curse. Jack heard a scream. That quivering blade had pierced one man's arm.

In the dark, Jack tripped and fell. He sprang up again just in time to see the sword dashed from the old man's hand. The attackers rushed in, and the next instant Jack was among them like a wild bull.

His first blow sent one of the attackers to the ground. He grabbed another by the shoulder, spun him around, and sent him tumbling to the pavement with a right cross. He tripped the third assailant, pushed him the ground, and planted a powerful kick to the man's stomach.

Then Jack felt his throat seized from behind in an iron grip and he was flung against the brick wall. Suddenly a loud report rang through the street, and a scream answered it. The clutch on Jack's throat relaxed.

Footsteps rang again, shouts drifted through the night and dogs bayed. A hand touched Jack's. He turned to see the old man, smoking pistol in one hand.

"Make a run for it, lad. It will do neither of us any good to be caught here. That's the police. Follow me; I know all the streets. Nobody but a fool gets mixed up with the police."

Utterly bewildered, Jack hurried after the old man. Police whistles were answering each other. Luckily they were moving through badly lit streets full of warehouses and offices. Jack wondered vaguely why they were running away. It was a clear case of self-defense, but this whole night seemed to be full of madness. He half expected to wake up presently on his barge and find it all a dream. It crossed his mind that, in his excitement, he might have made a terrible blunder. What if the people he had been using his fists upon were the old man's keepers? What if he had aided and abetted a dangerous lunatic to escape?

"Quicker, lad, quicker," urged the old man, even though Jack was having some difficulty keeping up with him.

It struck Jack, even in the excitement of their flight, that the old man's voice had lost its ring of command.

The old man turned into an alley. "This way, my lad, this way." Finally he slowed down. "Ah! we're safe. Give me your arm, for I'm a bit blown."

They passed under an archway, and all was dark. Jack could not see an inch ahead on either side. The old man leaned on his arm and began to chuckle softly, then struck a match. In its flickering light, Jack saw that they were in a small courtyard, walled in on three sides by dirty brick buildings. One of the buildings had expanded over the top of the courtyard, giving the area a wooden sky.

"By Blake and Drake and Nelson," he said peering into Jack's face with his beady, twinkling eyes, "your figurehead needs no painting. Don't be frightened. I'm sane and sober enough now. Perhaps I ought to send you away. Where do you live?"

"On the *Etruria*, anchored in the river, but I don't have a way to get back ..."

"Ah, yes, I'd forgotten. Come with me, then, lad. Be careful how you go up the ladder. I'd better go first with the candle."

Jack's head was still in a whirl. He watched the old man with knee breeches and trailing sword move to a pile of crates. A candle flared and guttered and pushed back some of the gloom. Then he mounted neither ladder nor stairs, but ratlines, a rope ladder that once belonged on a ship, which were hanging down the opposite wall. It was enough and more than enough to make Jack think it was all a dream. The old man pushed open a trapdoor at the top, and climbed through to the floor above. Jack nimbly followed up the ratline.

"Home at last, lad, home at last."

The trapdoor opened into a narrow hallway with only one door, now opened at the far end. Jack shut the trapdoor and stepped through the door.

The room Jack entered suited the man. The first object that met his view was a model of a fully-rigged three-decker hanging on the wall in a glass case. There were also skins of snakes, stuffed birds, carved elephant's tusks, shells, and gourds; dirks, cutlasses, flintlocks, dried alligator hides, shark's teeth, and a hundred other curios such as sailors love to gather. A fire blazed in the grate, and on either side of the hearth a couple of little carronades grinned at each other.

"Have ye killed Monkey Swayne, messmate?" croaked a voice so sepulchral and unearthly Jack shuddered.

"No, Jim, not yet," answered the old man.

"Slit his throat, slit his throat, messmate," croaked the voice. "Kill Monkey Swayne."

"Aye, aye, sir. We'll do it yet, Jim. We'll do it yet, never fear."

Jack looked around the room, and discovered the owner of the hideous voice was an ancient, mangy parrot, perched on one of the carronades. It tucked its head under one ragged wing and slumbered.

"What's your name, lad?" snapped out the old man in a way that suggested he was used to giving orders and having them followed.

"Drayton. Jack Drayton."

"Drayton, Drayton? Sink me, but I know the name. There was a Drayton with us at the battle of St. Vincent, when we pounded the French and Spaniards into splinters. He was a middy, and a bit of staunch timber. Dick Drayton his name, and a bright lad."

"My grandfather, Admiral Richard Drayton did fight at St. Vincent under Admiral Jervis," said Jack; "but what do you mean by saying —"

"Grandson of Dick Drayton, eh?" almost shrieked the old man. "Thunder and shrapnel! Let me feel your fist and look at ye. Sure enough, you've got Dick's eyes and chin. Ah! those were days! I saw his left wrist shot clean away, and he roared out to me: 'They've clipped off one of my fists, Juan, but the other is good enough to maul any six of 'em yet.' And, as I live, he was first aboard the Frencher that day."

Jack had heard the story of his grandfather's heroism before, and here, sitting opposite him, was a man who declared he had witnessed the incident with his own eyes. Could it be that he had really shared in the stirring sea-fights of long ago, or was it only the mania of a diseased mind?

"Have ye killed Monkey Swayne, messmate?" croaked the parrot, awakening from its dose.

"Not yet Jim, not yet."

"Slit his throat, slit his throat, messmate. Kill him!"

The old man put a bottle of rum and two glasses on the table. While Jack looked on in amazement, the old man placed a little crucible on the fire. The crucible contained lead. It quickly became molten. Jack's strange host deftly molded a dozen slugs, let them fall with a hiss into a bucket of water, and when they were sufficiently cool, he filed off the rough edges.

Then he loaded two pistols to the very muzzles, tightened the flints, primed the pans, and laid the great ugly weapons on the table beside the rum.

"Lad," he said suddenly, "ye said ye were poor. Are ye brave?"

"I believe that I am."

"Look me in the eyes. Ah, ye can do that without a flinch. When I was such a lad as you they whispered my name with white lips. Aye, they feared to speak it aloud. Even to this day it is not for-gotten. Shall I tell it ye?"

Jack didn't think he had any choice, so he nodded.

The old man leaned forward, his little black eyes glowing. "I am Black Juan Gaskara!"

CHAPTER TWO

Mad as a hatter.

J ack recognized the name of Black Juan Gaskara, freebooter and pirate, from one of the books he read in his uncle's library. No human fiend had ever slaughtered and robbed and ravaged as that monster of cruelty had done. His ship, the *Satan*, had pillaged from Charlestown to Trinadad. She was a phantom vessel and eluded every attempt to capture her. And then, towards the close of the year 1821, like a phantom she had vanished forever.

That the old man seated across the table from Jack was that man, that dreaded pirate, was an utter impossibility; he would have had to been born something like a hundred and ten years ago. Jack tried to hide a smile, but the man's twinkling eyes were too keen.

"So I'm mad, am I? I don't blame you for thinking it, but it's true. I am Black Juan Gaskara. Portuguese on my father's side, English on my mother's. Aye, and I fought well for England too, until a bragging officer struck me and I clapped a knife into his heart. The noose was round my neck, and the rope over the yardarm, but when the order came to run me up, the mutiny began. Every officer was shot, and the King's ship, *Macedon*, became the pirate vessel *Satan* that very day. That's history, my lad, that's history. Even Jim knows it."

The parrot opened its glassy eyes and laughed horribly.

"So how old are you?" ventured Jack.

"A-hundred and twelve, or maybe more, lad. Don't start and stare. In my time I've sent souls without number to Eternity, but Black Juan was no fool. He smoked little, and drank less, when all the others were swilling out their brains. And I lived on Peril Island, where every breath of air means another year of life, my lad. But I go mad at times like I was mad tonight. For twenty years I have been waiting for this. I'm doomed."

"Doomed, sir?"

"As good as dead." His voice sank. "It was fate. They've finally found me out. There's Samson Lake, Vanderlet, the Honorable, the Frenchy, and that demon Monkey Swayne. It may be a week before they murder me, it may be a month, it may be tonight. They'll do it, but I'll cheat 'em. They'll never win the secret." He opened a drawer in the table and pulled something out. "Here's the oath they've taken. I found it on old Lake's body when I shot him. Can ye read?"

"Of course I can read."

"Keep your powder dry, lad. Read it. Read it aloud."

It was a large piece of yellow linen that had been probably torn from a shirt. Some writing was upon it on both sides, very faded and difficult to decipher. Holding it near the light Jack read slowly, stumbling over the poor handwriting and archaic spellings:

Peril Island, June 1825. To my dear and only son, Harold Lake. Knowing that I am about to die, and that the fiend Gaskara will have no mercy, I place upon you the task of avenging your father's murder. The latitude and longitude of this beautiful and horrible place are both unknown to me. We were driven north for over eight months by a succession of hurricanes and storms that no vessel except this blood-stained and accursed ship could have weathered. For weeks we plunged through seas of crashing ice with the sky overhead crimson with flame. Eighty-seven men died, and fear killed them rather than scurvy, thirst, and hunger.

We had untold treasure on board, and every coin of it was steeped in human blood. While we were helpless specters, mere skin and bone, our accursed captain was lusty and strong. At last we mutinied and made a rush for the stores. He held the place against us single-handed, and shot nine of us. Desperate and mad with hunger and disease, the fifty of us who remained were about to scuttle the ship, when the icebergs vanished, and we sighted the paradise that Juan Gaskara has turned into a hell.

Jack looked up at the man calling himself Gaskara. He was slumped forward, his watery eyes seemingly focused somewhere in the past.

"Hell ... hell ..." The old man mumbled mournfully.

"Sir, if reading this is troubling you —"

The old man slapped the table with such force that Jack jumped. "Continue, lad, continue," he barked.

Jack returned to the text.

Heaven knows, my son, we were glad enough to land, but Black Juan remained behind. We had barely the strength to get out the four boats. He gave us muskets and powder. The island was lovely beyond all words, and we found fruits in abundance, but no game. Santley, our second in command, clubbed a seal, and we devoured it raw.

And then we plotted against the fiend who had starved us. We feared him as much as we hated him. We were all villains who had lived evil lives, and our souls were black with crime. We were armed, and Santley's plan was to row quietly back to the ship and shoot him down.

And now comes the greatest horror of all. It was a shark-infested sea. Santley led the way in the long boat, in which were sixteen men. A puff of smoke appeared against the Satan's black bulwarks, and a round shot crashed through the boat, which sank at once. Those shrieks are in my ears now. I see the tossing arms of my drowning comrades, the fins of the sharks, the blood red tinge that came into the water.

Then a charge of canister raked my own boat, and we rowed like demons. He meant to murder us all. Twenty men instead of one might have been manning the guns. After every shot he sprang upon the bulwarks and howled madly. We snapped down our flints at him, but no report followed. Gaskara had served us out charcoal instead of gunpowder!

I lost my head. The sea was alive with sharks. Helped by the fiend his master—for without Satan's help no mortal man could have done it unaided — Gaskara brought the vessel round and fired at us with the larboard guns. He sank every boat and even the voracious sharks were glutted.

Here are the names of those who reached the shore: Jacques Guerin, myself, Ephraim Vanderlet, Santley, and Little Dick Swayne, the dwarf — five in all. Santley was shot in the jaw and died that same night. We fled into the thick woods, for we knew that the lust of gold had turned Black Juan into a madman, and that he would pursue relentlessly.

Again, Jack glanced at the old man. He was nodding sadly. He realized that Jack had stopped reading again, and he gestured for him to keep going. It was as if hearing this account served as some kind of penance for the old man. Jack went on.

Two days afterwards Guerin went to the spring for water. He never came back. I found him lying face downwards there. Shot through the heart. Three unarmed men alone remained out of the whole crew of the accursed Satan.

We all had sons at home. Dick Swayne, a monster hardly less cruel than Gaskara, had appointed himself our leader. It was Swayne who suggested, when we thought ourselves doomed, to write down what had happened. Why, I know not, for we had no hope of escape. The murder of Guerin turned our hearts to water, and we moved to the other side of the island.

Here, a week later, we found a little cockleshell of a canoe of native make, washed up on the beach. That night Vanderlet went mad and ran shrieking through the woods. He came back no more, and then, as the boat would only hold one, Swayne and I cast lots. He won. We loaded the little craft with fruits and water, and rigged a sail of palm leaves.

I watched him as he sailed away over the unknown seas, and I was alone.

My son, I have made six copies of this my last writing on earth. Four, fastened with clay in hollow nuts, I have tossed into the sea, one I keep, one Swayne has taken with him. I know that I am very close to death. If Black Juan escapes, and this should ever fall into your hands, my dying command to you is to hunt him down. Even now he may be creeping upon me. Only an hour ago I think heard him moving through the woods.

And of the accursed, blood-stained gold for which we have murdered so many, and for which we are being in turn justly murdered — touch it not. He cannot work the ship alone, and he cannot carry away such wealth. He will bury it here, hoping to escape and return in another vessel whose crew will not know the secret.

Some day, if Heaven so wills, a good man will find this vast treasure and use it only for a good purpose. Such is my wish and prayer. It has cost me my life, and mayhap my soul. But touch it not, for in your hands it will turn only to sorrow and evil. It is the price of blood: Hunt down Black Juan Gaskara and avenge your father. — Seth Lake.

To my son, Harold Lake, at the Gunwale Inn, Portsmouth, England.

The old man had fallen asleep before Jack had time to finish reading the extraordinary document. Was the thing real or a forgery? It seemed real enough, and his strange host had spoken of men who had certainly lived. The names of Juan Gaskara and his lieutenant Santley were connected with many a deed of horror. They were almost as infamous as that of the Pirate Kidd.

The black eyes opened and glared stonily around. The old man leaped to his feet. His voice rang out strong and lusty:

"Sail-ho! Out with every scrap of calico, ye lazy dogs. Stave in a keg and fill yourselves with rum. There's red gold there, my imps of Satan. Curse ye, Santley, where are ye skulking? Try her now, Swayne, and put a chain-shot into her spars! Prettily done, prettily done! Up with the Roger and out with the plank! No quarter, lads, no quarter! A handful of guineas to the first man aboard her."

Jack drew back in his seat. What vision was burning in the old man's brain? His eyes were vacant. His wild talk made Jack nervous, but it was not the anxiety of possibly facing a maniac. There was something horribly uncanny and truthful in the way he called on those men so long dead to attack the merchantmen whose bones lay fathoms deep.

The old man dropped back into the chair. Jack slipped the piece of linen into his pocket without thought. Presuming that what he had read was not a myth, then no more bloodthirsty or more cruel monster had ever disgraced the earth than the man before him.

He remembered the strange people who had visited the barge. He recalled the word "Honorable" spoken by the dwarf, and the old man had mentioned that name too. And Swayne? The men who had formed the crew of the Satan were, of course, dead and forgotten. Did the strange vendetta still live, and were these mysterious people the sons or the grandsons of the murdered pirates of nearly eighty years ago?

But could this man seated in front of him actually be Black Juan Gaskara? How could he be? Before Jack could credit that he needed a more convincing proof.

The old man was awake again.

"I know, lad, ye doubt. Then look at this. Perhaps ye'll believe yer own eyes."

He pulled up his ruffed sleeve, disclosing a thin but sinewy arm. On it was tattooed in blue a skull and crossbones above the picture of a ship. Below were the words: "Juan Gaskara, Port Royal, February 9th, 1819. Done here by me, Ephraim Vanderlet." Then came a scroll with a blowing whale at each corner, and then a few lines of the weird song that still rang in Jack's ears: *A merry life, a short life, a noose for you and me, And Davy Jones must have our bones, if they call it piracy.*

Jack did not speak. Some strange influence seemed to be working upon him.

"You have told me a most amazing story," he said tentatively. "I don't … don't know what to believe."

"Easy, lad, easy. Never try to tack in a strong cross current with the wind abeam. Ye cannot put a big ball in a small gun," the old man cautioned.

"You tell me that you are Black Juan Gaskara —"

"I tell ye I am Black Juan Gaskara."

Jack held up one hand. "Fine. I will take it as read. You are Black Juan Gaskara. You amassed a treasure …"

"Aye, tis a king's ransom."

"You hid this treasure in a place called Peril Island."

"Aye, that be the truth."

"Science had made the earth such a tiny place," Jack reasoned, "that it seems impossible for an undiscovered island to exist."

"Ye have traveled the seas," the man calling himself Gaskara replied. "Ye know how vast they are. The world may be 'tiny,' as ye say, but there are spots still hidden from the prying eyes of man. Peril Island is such a spot."

"Fine. You supposedly have this huge treasure, worth millions perhaps, but yet you are living like this ..." Jack gestured around the cramped, dingy room.

The old man nodded sadly. "Aye. Heaven's curse is upon me. I killed all of the dogs, left the *Satan* to rot and hid the treasure on Peril Island. And there it lies today. I tried to sail south from Peril Island alone in the one boat left. Twenty, fifty, a thousand times I tried to escape, but the moment I got afloat, a gale was sure to rise. No ship ever came near that desolate rock, and my only companion was that bird. I gave up trying to count time. I longed to die, but I could not. Instead of growing weaker, I grew stronger as the years passed. Finally, I made it off the island and sailed south. 'Twould be little use to tell ye the rest, afore some whalers picked me up. They had stories of another small man who was in another port hundreds of miles away."

"I knew that man could only be Dick Swayne, and while he lived my secret was not safe. I set off to kill him, but when I reached the port I found that he had left. Trying to return, I was driven south again and was stranded on another island.

"One day a fishing craft came in sight. They carried me to the place Norway, and I stayed with them for a long time.

You may guess, lad, how I felt when I found that between burying the treasure and ending up in that fishing village, it had been forty-seven years."

Jack didn't say anything. What could all this be except the wild delusion of a madman's brain? But yet ...

"I tell ye," the old man went on, ignoring Jack's silence, "all Europe rang with the story; but they little knew I was Black Juan Gaskara. But Fate knew. In Lisbon I nearly died with fear when I stumbled up against Dick Swayne. At least, it was his ghost, and he knew me, I fled, but I can't escape — can't — can't!"

"And was it Dick Swayne?"

"Aye!" hissed the old man. "Dick Swayne come back to earth again. The curse is on me, the vendetta lives. They'll kill me; but I'll cheat the dogs, I'll cheat 'em. You shall have the secret, not they. Ha, ha, ha, ha —" His wild laugh died away in a choked gasp of horror. He went white with fear. "Whisht! What was that, lad?"

Hollow footfalls sounded out below. Gaskara stood up, trembling in every limb, and seized a pistol.

"Kill Dick Swayne," croaked the parrot. "Slit his throat, my merry dogs. Dicky, messmates."

And then silence fell. It was broken by the creak of the trapdoor opening in the hall. Footsteps approached the closed door, and a hoarse, uneasy breathing came from beyond it.

"Who's there?" Gaskara cried out.

Again came the noise of hollow footfalls slowly retreating, and the closing of the trapdoor. Then faintly through the damp night sounded the chorus:

> *"Dead men, live men, drink and gold,*
> *Yo-heave-ho! and they call it piracy,*
> *With the Roger at the truck —"*

The old man uttered a shrill cry, half laugh, half scream, dropped the great ugly pistol, and fell forward across the table. The parrot was croaking and screaming, but the old man did not stir.

Jack shivered. The rain lashed against the shuttered windows, the breeze wailed and moaned through the chimneys.

CHAPTER THREE

Jack had tough nerves, or thought he had tough nerves, but they were now unstrung. Even against his every sense of reason, he was beginning to think that the story of murder and horror he had listened to and read was built on a foundation of truth. For some mysterious cause this man was being dogged and hunted. His wild challenge had been accepted by the ruffians.

We kill him the chance is gone.

The words Jack had heard from one of the attackers as he ran to assist buzzed in his ears. The old man, then, must hold some secret which the brutes knew would be lost to them if they killed him.

Jack raised the limp form of the old man, then recoiled with a thrill of horror and repulsion. Juan Gaskara had only swooned, but the white face had changed terribly. It was furrowed with a thousand wrinkles, and pouched and baggy under the eyes.

Jack did not doubt his age now. He might have been centuries old.

He unfastened the frills and bared Gaskara's chest in order to feel how his heart beat. There was more tattooing there — the King's broad arrow, and the words, "Juan Gaskara, boatswain, H.M.S. Sybil, 1804."

Here was another startling proof of the truth of the incredible story. The tattooing was done roughly, as an unskilled sailor might do it, and the color suggested that gunpowder had been used. Jack poured a little rum down the man's throat and chafed his hands.

This district was unknown to Jack; if he ventured out in search of a doctor, the chances wore that he would never find his way back again. Trying to return to his barge in the dark, even if he could find his way, could possibly leave him open to attack by the others. He had no choice but to stay. He thought of trying to arouse some of the neighbors — if there were indeed any neighbors around this forsaken place — but a subtle, intangible sense of lurking danger kept him from drawing back to the heavy bolt of the door. He could do no more, nothing except wait.

Once or twice he thought he heard the same hoarse sound of heavy breathing. The parrot chattered and laughed and scraped its beak on the little carronade.

Jack sat with his chin in his hand. He was convinced now that the shriveled, silent figure before him was Black Juan Gaskara. Wild, idiotic, impossible as it seemed, all his doubts had vanished. That caused him to be calmer, somehow, and allowed him to reason more clearly. Suddenly he sprang up.

Some other living, breathing presence was close at hand.

He could hear nothing, see nothing, but he sensed it. He stood rigid and strained every nerve to listen. The feeling of being watched and dogged slowly passed away. With a soft, but nervous, laugh, he sat down again. He took out the scrap of linen, and once more read the gruesome story of the fate of the crew of the vessel *Satan*.

Could it be true? Did Peril Island exist? If so, by what name was it known to modern navigators? If it is even known now? The ice and the sky "crimson with flame" suggested the northern regions, perhaps volcanic ones. And then one clause in the dead man's handwriting riveted his attention:

Some day, if Heaven wills, a good man will find this vast treasure and use it only for a good purpose. Such is my wish and prayer. It has cost me my life, and mayhap my soul. But touch it not, for in your hands it will only turn to sorrow and evil. It is the price of blood —

A heavy fist beat against the door. Jack jumped up.

"Who's there?" Jack's hand mechanically clutched the big pistol. He stood. "Answer me! Who is there?" he cried more loudly.

"Curses!" growled a voice. "He's not alone!"

"Most likely the swab who helped him. Break down the door and wring his neck!" came a second voice.

"Stand aside, then. Show a light, Monkey," added a third voice.

There was a thudding crash, and the stout door shook under the weight of a heavy body. Every muscle in Jack's frame began to tighten. These birds of prey of the night meant no good to the old man. Murderer or no murderer, pirate or no pirate, he was helpless now, and Jack simply couldn't give him up to those villains on the other side of the door. The ruffians also knew Jack had helped the old man escape from them and could possibly identify them; now Jack's fate was completely intertwined with the old man's.

"Gently, please!" said Jack, surprising himself at how calmly he spoke. "Keep away from the door. Surely you remember how effective the pistol was earlier this evening? I've got two aimed at the door at this very minute, and they are loaded."

He heard angry oaths, then a voice growled, "Mate, if you'll take good advice, you'll get out of this, and mind your own concerns. We don't mean you no harm, but you're working in a proper way to get six inches of knife in your chest. Open the door, and we'll let you go."

Jack didn't believe that for a moment. They simply were not the kind of men who would pat him on the head and send him on his merry little way if he let them in, no matter what pledges or promises they gave.

"Tell me what you want," Jack demanded.

"We want Juan Gaskara."

"Then return at a proper hour," replied Jack, almost as if he was a secretary, "for you will see no one here tonight."

They began to mutter. He recognized the odd drawl of the "Honorable," and the harsh, cracked tones of "Monkey" Swayne, the visitors to his barge from earlier that night.

"Then you won't let us in?" asked a voice.

"No," Jack replied firmly.

There was more hoarse muttering and whispers.

"Chance it!" growled one voice.

"It's too risky. Too much noise will bring the police," put in another voice.

Again a human body hurled itself against the panels. This was followed by a conference among the voices, followed by the creak of the trapdoor.

"Then let me talk to him. He, he, he!" It was Monkey Swayne. "Are you listenin', my handsome bantam cock? Come out before you get your neck wrung. You've seen me once tonight and admired my beauty. You're settin' on a barrel of gunpowder, and we've got hold of the fuse. Open the door. We don't want to hurt the old man. Sink me! We're messmates of him! Will you open the door?"

"I grow weary of repeating myself. No."

For the third time, the door shook and trembled.

"If you do that again," Jack called out, "I shall shoot. The law is on our side. We are threatened, and the law gives us the right to protect ourselves. Besides, the corridor is narrow. Before I get six inches of knife in my chest, as you so colorfully put it, I will make sure to take a couple of you with me. I shall not warn you again."

A sudden blast of cold air struck him. Jack glanced up toward its source: the dormer window, located high in one wall. The window stood open, and a figure crouched in the frame. The figure raised his arm, and something silver flashed toward Jack.

Jack dodged to one side, a dull thud coming from the table behind him. He fired his gun at the window, and the figure disappeared. Jack checked in back of him. A knife quivered in the table.

"Curse that shot!" said a voice from the hallway. "That will bring the police again!"

"Well, allow me to make sure of that!" called Jack. He picked up a bottle and threw it out the open window. It smashed against the pavement with a satisfying loud crash. He yelled at the top of his lungs. "Fire! Fire! Help! Murder Murder!"

A police whistle pierced the blackness of the night. Jack grabbed the second pistol and fired it straight at the door. The bullet splintered through a part of the wood. Surprised curses and the sound of bodies hitting the floor filled the hallway. A second and third police whistle sounded, closer this time.

"It sounds like the police are gathering around," Jack said. "I think it is about time for you to take your leave."

"All right, mate," croaked Swayne, "we'll sheer off. You win this battle. But if some fine night you got a knife rammed into you, don't blame us. We'll carve you up, don't fret. He, he, he! Good night! We'll take the liberty of burning your lovely barge on the way back, won't we, mates?"

"We'll cut the thing adrift and let it blaze. It's a fine idea, Monkey."

Jack paled. Could they mean it? Was it only a jest? If they burned the barge and turned it adrift, he would lose everything. He bit his lips, and his eyes grew haggard.

He heard them at the bottom of the ratlines. Perhaps there was still time to make terms and open the door. He made a move for the door.

There was a snarl behind him. Juan Gaskara was out of his chair. He drew his sword, and shoved Jack out of the way. The old man wrenched back the bolts on the door, and sprang into the darkness. Jack heard a chorus of angry voices, then running feet. Then the door was closed again and barred by Gaskara.

With shaking hand, the old man began to reload the pistols.

"Stand by me, lad," he cried, "and I'll make you rich for life. I'll cheat 'ems. I'll cheat 'ems. Ha, ha, ha! Stand by Black Juan, and he'll show Dick Drayton's grandson where he can dig out gold like clay. Swear you'll not leave me."

The old man sat, buried his face in his arms and slumbered.

Jack knew he couldn't leave the old man until morning at least, or he could be at the receiving end of another knife. He sat with unblinking eyes and strained ears until the night of horror was past, starting at every little creak or groan of the old building's timbers.

CHAPTER FOUR

There is a vast difference between darkness and the broad, honest light of day. Gaskara's story, the wild vendetta, the rag that contained the supposed declaration of Seth Lake, Peril Island itself — all that had seemed real in the shadowy realm of night had now become simply a dream. Jack was alone in the odd room and he could laugh at it all. Gaskara was a madman, and nothing more.

"Tumble up, ye skulking lubbers, tumble up!"

"Aye aye, sir," shrilled out the parrot.

Jack was not alone as he had fancied. The wrinkled face of the old man rose over the edge of the hammock.

"What d'ye make of it, Monkey? A King's ship, d'ye think? A King's ship it is. Sink me, we'll wind her and rake her as we go. He, he, he! Double shot the guns, you skulkers. Vanderlet, take the helm. Ye wild dogs, ye merry dogs, rip the spars out of her and I'll swim ye in rum."

"Aye, aye, sir," cackled the parrot.

Jack seized the old man's shoulder and shook him. Reason dawned again in the black eyes.

"Is it you, lad, is it you?" said Juan Gaskara. "I was dreamin' of the day we led the King's frigate. Chain shot! Such a merry dance. Sink me, the *Satan* could run as well as fight. Run, lad! She was the fastest vessel afloat in any breeze."

"I must leave you," said Jack. He needed to get away to think it all over.

Gaskara gripped Jack's arm tightly. "Leave me, lad! Surely not; you wouldn't break your word. Didn't you promise not to leave me?"

Jack gently pried Gaskara's grip loose. "I said I would not leave you while you were in danger, sir."

"I'm always in danger," gasped Gaskara hoarsely. "Perhaps it's less perilous for me by day than night, for evil beasts are night prowlers, lad. And didn't ye say ye had no home? Sink me, but I'll keep gallant Drayton's grandson to his word." And then his voice vibrated with terror as he added. "For the love of pity, lad, don't leave a doomed man. I'm not ready to slip my cable yet."

Jack backed a couple of steps away from the hammock. He was starting to believe again this man was really Black Juan Gaskara, but the story about the treasure, that's the stuff of penny dreadfuls. Then why were those others after the old man? Jack's curiosity was aroused, as when it led him to explore the winding back streets of the ports in which his liner docked, and occasionally ending up in parts of town where he probably shouldn't have been.

A legendary treasure located on an unknown island, however, wouldn't fill Jack's belly or pay for his upkeep at the moment. That required a more mundane approach with the White Star Line.

"I will not break my word, sir," he answered, "but I must go for a few hours, at least."

"But ye'll come back, ye'll come back?" Gaskara implored.

For a once feared and deadly pirate, Gaskara's pleading was almost heartbreaking. "Of course. As soon as I am able."

The old man sprang out of the hammock. "D'ye want money?"

Of course, I do, thought Jack. But he wasn't about to take money from the old man. "No, thank you all the same."

"But ye'll take the bearings well," said Gaskara eagerly, "so as not to enter the wrong channel. And when ye come knock four times. I'll sing out 'Satan,' and ye'll answer 'Peril Island.'"

"I understand. I will," said Jack.

"Good luck go with ye," said Juan Gaskara sadly, "for I may never see your trim figure-head more."

He held out his shriveled hand. To Jack it felt like ice. Then holding one of the great pistols in readiness, Gaskara cautiously opened the door.

"Not a sail in sight," he muttered. "Make good speed, lad, and a prosperous v'yage. Ye'll come back, ye're sure of that?"

"Without fail! You can count on that."

Jack smiled and went into the hallway, the door closing behind him. He heard the latches rasp into place. He opened the trapdoor then climbed down the swaying ratlines into the courtyard. He passed under the dark archway and stepped outside.

He could hardly believe that London owned such a desolate, dilapidated spot. It was an abandoned wharf, with many of the structures on it in ruins or very close to it. A few of the buildings had forlorn "To Let" signs posted on them, perhaps the only things holding up the walls. The only outpost of life in this wasteland came from the building next to the one he had just left: a dingy warehouse with an illegible and faded name painted over the filthy windows. Its loading doors stood open, like a gaping maw, and from inside came shouted orders and the scrapping of crates being dragged across the floor. The presence of workers so near

Gaskara's hideout would certainly stop Swayne and the others from trying something during the day, at least.

A streak of black, greasy water separated it from a second wharf even more dilapidated. A wooden bridge with a worm-eaten rail spanned the water. It creaked ominously as Jack crossed it.

He made a rough plan of the way as he went along. At last he reached familiar ground. It was past eleven o'clock. He was nervous, too, about the barge, but to his relief he saw it floating in the sunshine. At least the toughs hadn't gone through with their threats. Yet.

He still hadn't eaten, and was starving. He couldn't worry anymore about Gaskara or his future, or pretty much anything else, on a completely empty stomach. He turned into a little eating house and made a frugal meal. After he ate, he stepped outside, looking regretfully at the paltry store of money that remained.

"A collar, and a shave we must have," Jack said to himself, "then change into my other suit, then walk every inch of the way to the White Star offices on Cockspur Street. I should be back in time to return to Gaskara."

He began walking toward Lucknan's Wharf. He had to think about what to do about the old man who called himself Juan Gaskara. If he went to the police, then he'd be involved in the fracas … at any rate, the old man didn't expect him to return for a few hours. That was enough time to complete his business at hand, and try to think of a plan.

"Oh, steward!"

The voice intruded into his thoughts, and he found himself reacting to the word like an automaton, turning toward the summons by habit.

Another young man, not much older than Jack, stood a short distance away. He was slightly shorter, husky, with a muscular physique that spoke to years of physical labor.

"Yes, you, steward," the youth put on a posh accent. "My friend seems to have vomited all over everything. It's really a frightful mess. Hop to it and clean it up, that's a good lad."

Jack broke out in a huge grin. "Hector! Hector Dane!" The two embraced, pounding each other on their backs. They broke apart with a handshake. "It's good to see you again! I thought you had signed on for that voyage on the *Adriatic*. I looked for you onboard but couldn't find you. What in the world are you doing here?"

"I slung my hook from being a trimmer. A year and a half was enough for shoveling coal." Hector took off his cap and pointed to his sandy blonde hair. "I still can't get that infernal dust out of my hair!"

He snapped the cap back on. "So off I went to Cornwall to fish, and spent some time above decks for a change. At least, until the captain took sick."

Jack was a 16-year-old deck steward serving on his initial voyage when he first met Hector. He had rounded the corner of the crew deck and encountered him. Jack was taken aback at first. Hector looked like an escapee from the underworld: stripped to the waist, streaked by filthy rivulets of sweat and coal dust from working in the boiler room. Except his hands were clean, and holding a book on philosophy he was reading.

They started talking about the book, with Jack discovering they were both voracious readers. Hector had a curious and active mind, with a prodigious memory for what he read; not what Jack would normally expect from somebody who spent long, hot hours hauling heavy wagon loads of coal from the storage lockers to the ship's boilers. The two became friends over their love of reading, with Jack smuggling books to Hector from the passengers' library, and Hector teaching Jack self-defense and physical culture. Over the next two years, they frequently found themselves on the same ship, sometimes rooming with each other between voyages, simply picking up their friendship where they had left off.

"You look very off luck, Jack." Hector's hand swept up and down Jack's attire. "Clothes like that are long gone. Not smart. I guess you haven't crawled back to your uncle?"

"That crusty, ill-tempered, gout-tormented old —" Jack waved off the rest of the sentence. "No. And hopefully after two years, he has stopped sending people to hunt for me." Jack imitated his uncle's gruff voice and shook his fist. "No one ever walks out on me, my lad!"

"Except you."

"Except me."

"You're a sticker. I would have been greatly disappointed in you if you had gone back," said Hector. "What have you been doing with yourself?"

"The *Adriatic* was my last ship," Jack said. "She was a good ship, but I wanted to see what it was like to stay in one place for a while."

"And? What's it like then?" Hector folded his arms and cocked his head, a bemused expression on his face as though already knowing the story's outcome.

"For a few dismal weeks I earned a small salary working in an even smaller room as a weighing-office clerk at one of the coal wharves. Then I discovered that the coal companies were charging the shipping lines for more coal than they actually carried in the barges."

"It's a common practice."

"A common practice, maybe, but it still doesn't make it right. Anyway, I went to my boss to complain, and the discussion became, shall we say, heated ..." Jack shrugged off the rest of the sentence.

"And you were discharged," Hector finished.

"That is stating it politely. I not only got the chuck, but was almost thrown down the stairs for good measure." Jack shrugged. "I guess back to sea I go. I was planning on visiting the White Star Line offices to sign up for a ship."

"Where do you kip?"

Jack pointed to the *Etruria*. "I live on that barge."

"It is a little bit of a doss house," Hector said.

Jack chuckled. "Perhaps. It is the result from being the smoking-room steward on the *Adriatic*."

"Smoking-room steward, eh?" Hector nodded approvingly. "You rose through the ranks fast for such a young lad."

Jack laughed. "It was due to my sparkling personality and my complete discretion. Anyway, Lord Graydon Garth took to me and learned I hadn't a proper place to live between voyages. So the *Etruria* was his end of voyage tip to me. I would have preferred the cash naturally, but still, shouldn't look a gift horse in the mouth and all that. I'm glad to have her now, since the change purse is very light."

Hector thought a moment. "Well, now you've got a crew mate."

"But, Hector, it's madness. I've got no money."

"I've got plenty," said Hector, patting one pocket. It jingled with coin. "The old fisherman paid me for the last season. Which probably was his last season, as well."

"But, Hector, look here —"

"Can't look. I'm blind." Hector folded his arms.

Jack gave it up. It was useless to argue. He knew Hector's stubborn nature too well. He grinned and stuck out his hand. "Welcome aboard."

"Now, how are you stocked with provisions?"

Jack shook his head. "I'm not."

"Hmm. Shops?"

"Hector, I can't take —"

"Shops." It was a command.

Jack saluted and smiled. "Aye aye, sir. This way, sir."

In due time Jack and Hector returned to the wharf, carrying innumerable provisions. Hector raised his arm to signal for a waterman. Jack stopped him.

"No, I'm looking for a specific one ... there, there he is." Jack whistled and called out: "Marsden!"

Marsden, the waterman well known to Jack, was plying his oars not far away. He rowed toward the wharf.

"Marsden's a good man," Jack said to Hector. "He doesn't take you halfway to your destination then demand double the fare, and threaten to dump you in the river if you won't pay it. And he accepts my credit."

Jack and Marsden exchanged greetings as the waterman reached the wharf. "What have you done with your own tub — sold it?" asked Marsden.

"Some brutes cut it adrift last night," Jack replied as he and Hector climbed in.

"I'll keep my eyes open for it," offered Marsden.

"Thank you, Marsden. I'd appreciate that."

Jack introduced Hector, and Marsden started rowing his boat toward the *Etruria*.

"Marsden," asked Jack, "in your travels, have you seen an older gent around, dressed in buckled shoes, knee-breeches, and a coat with wide lappets and laced cuffs?"

"Where's he off to? A fancy dress ball?" snorted Marsden.

Jack laughed. "Perhaps. Well, have you seen somebody like that?"

Marsden shook his head. "No, mate, it sounds like nobody I've seen."

"Who is that you're talking about?" asked Hector.

"Somebody I encountered last night," answered Jack.

"Somebody dressed like that around here?" Hector asked in astonishment.

"I'll tell you about it later," said Jack.

"Here we are," Marsden said when they reached the *Etruria*. Before Jack could say anything, he continued, "I don't want anything from you. I know your funds are low."

"No, no, no," Hector cried as he pulled out some coin. "How much is his tab, including this carriage?"

"Hector, I can't —," Jack started.

"Hush, you," Hector said to Jack, then turned his attention back to Marsden. "Well, how much is the grand total?"

Hector paid off Marsden, along with a nice tip, and joined Jack on deck.

"Hector, I don't know what to say ..."

"Then just shut it," Hector said. "Let's go to the cabin."

The two entered the tiny cabin. Hector put down his packages, looked about the small, untidy space, the broken window, then at Jack.

Jack shrugged. "Maid's day off."

"Several days off, truth be told. It looks like a bear pit. Seems like you could use a second chair, some crockery, a piece of glass to mend the window, some coal and some paraffin oil."

"Hector, I can't have you keep spending your money on me, old chap," protested Jack.

"How are you going to stop me, steward?" Hector threw a couple of punches in Jack's direction. "Remember, I'm still a better boxer than you."

Jack spread his arms wide and grinned. "I concede."

"Good." Hector lit the paraffin stove and set the skillet on the burner, while Jack started to put away the rest of the purchases. A boat rasping against the side of the barge interrupted them.

"Wonder if the cub's at home, dear boys," drawled a voice that made Jack spring up.

"I'll see, my darlings, I'll see," croaked another voice.

The next moment a distorted figure was squatting on the narrow sill and the ugly face of Monkey Swayne leered and grinned at them.

"Two of 'em," Swayne called over his shoulder, "and there's one new. Good-day to you, my bonnie pets. Two of 'em, Honorable, I say."

"Bai Jove, are there really, Monkey?" came a voice from outside. "Dear me, that's one too many. Strangle the new one, dear boy."

"Say, you, trash, you ain't wanted here," he cronked, pointing at Hector. "My business ain't with you. Clear out or I'll tickle your ribs with a nine inch piece of knife. He, he, he!"

Hector shot the hot skillet at the leering imp. It struck the Swayne between the eyes and flung him backwards through the window. There was a howl, followed by a splash and a volley of curses.

"Well played," commented Jack.

"Thank you," replied Hector.

"But that was my only skillet."

"I'll buy you a new one."

Jack and Hector bounded on deck. The tide was running fast and a black head was dancing down the stream. A boat with four men in it was in pursuit. In the bow, boat-hook in hand, stood a tall frock-coated top-hatted man. He thrust the boat-hook forward and the bony fingers of Monkey Swayne clutched it. He was dragged on board, limp and dripping. Then the boat was pulled round.

The boat came nearer and Jack snatched up a mop, the only thing faintly resembling a weapon he could find. The one pulled from the river, blood rushing from his nostrils, was dancing, cursing, and raving for revenge. Jack set his teeth grimly.

"Ahoy, you there!" shouted the Honorable.

"Board him, board him!" screamed Monkey Swayne. "Burn you, I'll have your life for this! I'll make you suffer for this!"

He hurled the spiked boat-hook with all his strength. It buzzed over Jack's head. The boat shot nearer.

"Kill 'em! Kill 'em both!" yelled Swayne, "there's nobody about."

The oars ceased to thrash the water.

"Police, lads," cried the Honorable.

A launch manned by a crew of Thames police came puffing swiftly down the stream. The Honorable's boat pulled away.

"Burn you both, I'll get you yet!" roared Monkey Swayne.

The boat pulled across the black wide river, and the wild chorus came faintly over the water:

> "Yo-heave-ho, there's lots of gold at sea,
> A merry life, a short life, a noose for you and me;
> And Davy Jones must have our bones,
> if they call it piracy!"

Hector glanced at the mop in Jack's hand. "What did you plan to do with that? Scrub them down?"

Jack grinned ruefully. "It was the only thing handy."

"Should we hail the police?"

"No, those blackguards will be lost among the docked vessels before the police get here." Jack dropped the mop to the deck.

"Who are those brutes, Jack? They're certainly not friends of yours. What does it all mean?" Hector asked.

Jack was silent for a second before he answered quietly. "Unfortunately, I think I know exactly what it means. It involves an older gent, dressed in buckled shoes, knee-breeches, and a coat with wide lappets and laced cuffs."

CHAPTER FIVE

"**W**hat a staggering yarn!" Hector leaned back in the chair, tossing the scrap of linen containing the story on the table. He let out a slow whistle and picked up a hot mug of tea. "It is something that Robert Louis Stevenson would have written. A hundred and twenty or thirty years old pirate?"

"Black Juan Gaskara, to be specific." Jack sat in the lower bunk, and sipped his tea. He shook his head in amazement. "I'm believing it is all true, astounding as it sounds. I met Black Juan Gaskara himself."

"Oh, he's off his chump, surely," Hector argued. "He couldn't possibly be Black Juan. As for the piracy, well, that's all lunacy."

"His tale is to a certain extent backed up by the statement written on the linen," Jack pointed out. "Surely you must agree that it is genuine."

"I agree that this linen is old, and possibly, perhaps probably, the tale written on it is true." Hector tapped on the fabric, then sipped some more tea. "The old man could have somehow obtained it, and in his own unbalanced mind, assumed the identity of Black Juan Gaskara. At least it is different than thinking you're Napoleon."

Jack shook his head. "If you had seen the tattoos, heard him speak ..."

"Well, if you are going to start believing lunatics —"

"I believe that one." Jack hopped off the bunk and went to the tea kettle. He poured himself another cup.

"He could be dangerous, and should be in restraints," Hector said.

"Hector, he's a tired, sick old man," Jack said. He remembered how well Gaskara handled himself during the brawl, but decided not to tell Hector. "I can't very well go to the coppers and say I know where they can arrest a 112-year-old pirate, now can I? I'd be laughed out of the station. Maybe I can talk him into seeing the authorities, or a doctor, or something."

"But why are those blackguards dogging him?" Hector asked. He thought for a second. "He must have some money and they've got wind of it. It can't be anything else."

"Most likely," Jack agreed, also not telling Hector about the supposed treasure. That would simply add more to his insanity argument. "All the more reason to get him help. Anyway, I'll get at the truth tonight."

Hector stood. He was incredulous. "Tonight? You're going back tonight? Why?"

"Because I promised."

"What about the White Star Line?"

"Hector, I've already walked out on one sick old, man. I don't intend to make it two," Jack shot back. He stopped, puzzled. That wasn't what he intended to say. He didn't even know why he said what he did. He continued in a mumble. "The White Star Line will always be there."

Hector didn't seem to notice. "Then I'm going with you."

Jack shook his head. "I appreciate it, Hector, but no. If he sees me with somebody else, he may cut it. Then I will never find him."

"I'll stay out of sight." Hector looked a little hurt.

"No," Jack said firmly. "It will only take me a couple of hours."

"What if those others show up?" Hector protested.

"Hector, you've taught me how to take care of myself, and you've taught me well. Remember that night on the docks in Capetown? Between the two of us, we disposed of those five hooligans."

"They were blotto."

"They had fists nonetheless. I promise I'll keep my eyes peeled. If anything seems remiss, I'll come back." Jack shrugged. "Besides, I can run faster than they can."

"I still don't like it," Hector groused.

"You worry like an old woman, Hector," Jack laughed. "Believe me, nothing will happen, and at least I'll come back with some interesting stories. Let's fix that window so that we don't have any more unexpected visitors popping in."

It was a quick trip to get some glass and replace the window. A few hours later, Jack left Hector to take care of the barge, and Marsden rowed him ashore. In spite of the care he had taken to impress the turnings and twistings of the various streets and alleys on his mind last night, he found himself thoroughly at sea. The fickle weather changed, and it was raining once more. Night was falling rapidly, and an upstream wind sent black oily waves rolling over the river. A mist swept over the water in bellowing clouds.

He looked about, hoping to meet someone from whom he could obtain information, but human beings seemed to shun this ruined, desolate place. Then he fancied he heard a stealthy footstep. Jack spun round and peered through the rain and gloom. He saw a shadowy figure gliding behind the rotting skeleton of a boat.

"Messmate," cried Jack, "hold hard a minute. I'm out of my bearings."

The figure glided back into view, and Jack strode forward. The man was short, black-haired and swarthy, and his left arm hung in a sling.

"Where you want to go, mate?" he asked.

"Crosskeys Lane," said Jack.

"On the right, on the left, on the left and on the right once more, and then you reach him."

"Much obliged," said Jack.

Jack leaped a low wall and gained a narrow lane. The way seemed unfamiliar. Jack went on, tightening his pea coat around himself to keep out the chill.

"Nice cheerful game this is," he muttered. "I've about had my fill of it."

The chill rain began to soak through Jack's clothes, and the slush penetrated his worn boots. The narrow streets were deserted. Only a few second floor windows glowed with feeble light leaking through cracked and torn blinds. He heard the harsh, demanding cry of a baby as he passed under one of them.

He turned to his right. No lights at all shone from any window, and the gray walls glistened from the rain, making Jack feel like he was walking among giant tombstones in a wet graveyard.

He walked down the middle of the street. Once or twice he fancied hearing footsteps behind him. He stopped, but heard nothing but the rain splashing on the pavement and gurgling down the gutters. Finally he reached the corner of Crosskeys Lane, marked by a barely legible sign.

"Safe in port at last, thank goodness," he said.

He knew the proper turning now. The dark arch loomed before him, and it was only a few strides to the strange old man's stranger quarters. A piercing whistle from behind almost deafened him. The next moment three men were upon him.

Jack went down, but with a mighty effort that sent one of his assailants reeling, he regained his feet, lashing out with his arms he began to roar for help. The archway cast such a dense shadow that he could not see his foes.

"Burn him, he'll have the police on us," parted an enraged voice. "Give him the knife and let the breath out of him."

"No, you fool, no! You've almost spoiled us already with your madness. If we're nabbed, the old hound'll set all sail. Hammer his teeth down his thr —"

The words ended in a thud and a sickly gurgle. Jack's fist had found the speaker's jaw and driven his head against the brickwork of the arch. A loop of material whipped around Jack's throat and tightened, almost strangling him. Gasping for air, his hands clutched at the cloth, desperately trying to loosen it.

"That's got it, Guerin," croaked Monkey Swayne. "Proper use of your sling. But don't stiff 'im yet. Where are you, Lake?"

A groan answered him, and Swayne answered the groan with a chuckle.

"Pasted yer, eh?" he grinned. "Serve yer right for hittin' his fist with yer face. Now, Honorable, show a glim and let's see what we've got."

A light shone out as the door on a dark lantern opened. The tall man in the frock-coat and top-hat man joined the group. He held the lantern high.

Another figure approached. It was Lake and he was pressing a blood-stained handkerchief to his lips.

"Clean him over," drawled the dandy, "and let us see what he's got."

Lake searched Jack's pockets. He only found a handkerchief, and a penny.

"Is that all?" growled the Honorable.

Swayne cursed and stamped on the handkerchief. Then he whipped out his knife.

"I won't have it, Monkey, bai jove. I just won't have it," the Honorable ordered.

The ogre spat in Jack's face and then looked up, his ferret eyes ablaze, at the dandy.

"Oh, yer won't, won't yer?" he challenged.

"That is right. I won't."

"Nor me neither," spluttered Sampson Lake, shoving his bloody handkerchief into his pocket. "Now I don't object to killin' when there's no risk, but when there is risk, I do. And risk there is, all through your foolery. You went mad in the pub last night. We almost got hauled off to the gaol."

"Ye idiots," Monkey Swayne snapped as he put away his knife, "d'ye think a man can only carry papers in his pockets! Hold a light."

He pulled Jack's coat open and thrust in his ugly hand. There was nothing. Swearing, he pawed open Jack's shirt and searched again. Again nothing.

"Gaskara hasn't parted," said Lake.

"It seems not, burn him," growled Monkey Swayne. "I'll get my clutch on him to-night or I'll know the reason why."

"Bai Jove, that's madness," answered the dandy. "I do not relish engaging Black Juan in that narrow hallway. He'll riddle you, dear boy. We need to lure him out in the open."

"Send him the sign, to get him outside," suggested Lake.

"How?"

"Why, on that rogue there."

Swayne muttered his evil chuckle. He dipped one crooked finger into the mud, and scrawled a cross on Jack's forehead, which he enclosed with double circles.

"He, he, he, he!" tittered Monkey Swayne. "He's had that little keepsake twice, and there's luck in odd numbers. If it was only killin', wouldn't it be easy? He, he, he! Sink the sly, old fox, there's no getting at him. We've run him to earth, and now we've got to dig him out. And we'll do it with this lad's help."

"Hist! Take care!" came the Frenchman's warning whisper. Lake clamped his hand over Jack's mouth.

Footfalls sounded, passed the month of the dark arch, and died away.

"That was a sensible fellow not to come in here," said the Honorable with a laugh.

"He, he, he, he, he! I'll bolt the rabbit," cackled Swayne. "Get out of sight, my bonnie rogues, if yer ain't lead-proof. Give 'em 'Satan's Song' when I tip the wink, and, by Davy Jones, I'll show your Black Juan Gaskara hisself. Could yer pink him, d'yer think, Honorable? You can hold a gun pretty straight."

"Good Lord! Do you take me for such a fool with what there is at stake?"

"It's a sight too risky to try," agreed Lake. "An inch too far might finish him and our chances with him."

"Suit yerselves," said Swayne. He motioned to Lake.

Lake stepped in front of Jack, grinned, and punched him in the stomach. The noose-like cloth loosened as he doubled over. Lake pulled Jack up by his hair and gut-punched him a second time. Jack dropped to the ground on all fours, then Lake's savage kick to his temple rolled him onto his side, striking his head on the pavement.

Jack entered a limbo world, somewhere between consciousness and not. His voice cracked in his throat, and the darkness swam with luminous spots. His mind and his body seemed disconnected, one not responding to the other.

They pulled Jack to his feet and dragged his semi-conscious body to near the ratlines.

"Bait the trap there," said Honorable.

They dumped Jack to the ground next to the ratlines.

"Pipe up, my merry larks, my nightin-gales, my black canaries," grinned Monkey Swayne. "Many a good man has gone fathoms deep to the music of that dear old tune. Softly, softly!"

His own shrill cracked treble joined in, and the wild song trembled on the damp air:

"Dead men, live men, drink and gold!
Yo-heave-ho! and they call it piracy.
With the Roger at the truck, yo-ho, my comrades bold,
Yo-heave ho! there's lot of gold at sea!"

Jack rolled on his back just as the trapdoor was dashed open. A brilliant beam of light streamed out. Through blurred vision he saw Juan Gaskara. In his knee-breeches and buckled shoes, cocked hat and queue, a naked blade in his right hand, and long-barreled flintlock in his left and another in his belt, a vision from the past appeared.

"Have at ye, curs, have at ye," he screamed. "I'll take the challenge. Curse ye, Monkey Swayne, curse ye, Lake and Vanderlet. I know where your fathers' bones bleach, I know who left 'em there to bleach. 'Twas Juan, old murderous, merciless Juan. And he did it for gold, for rich, red blood-stained gold. Have at ye, have at ye!"

"Kill Monkey Swayne, kill him, messmate. Slit his throat, slit his throat," croaked the eerie voice of the parrot from inside the room.

There was silence. The door opened wider and the light fell on the limp form of Jack Drayton. Jack shook his head, trying to clear it, and raised up one hand as a warning. Monkey Swayne stepped into the light.

Jack didn't know if it was a trick of the light, or his own woozy mental state, but Gaskara appeared younger, stronger. He truly was Black Juan Gaskara, the Juan whose name was only breathed with trembling lips on the wide seas from Charlestown to Trinidad. The thin arms were now strong and muscular. His face flushed with the vigor of youth. The eyes blazed with the love of a fight. He was the Juan of eighty years ago.

Gaskara tore out after the others brandishing his sword. Strength more than human had come back to his limbs; his eyes flashed murder, the wild oaths of a past century when seafarers feared neither God nor devil poured from his lips.

Then came a yell that none but a maniac could utter. The old man thrust the pistol into his belt, fairly slid down the ratlines, and dived into the courtyard. He drew his gleaming sword and waved it. His cracked voice shrilled through the night in fierce defiance.

Even Swayne recoiled in utter dread. The rogues backed away, chilled with pale fear. Lake uttered a scream as Gaskara's steel pricked his arm. The four men fled as if some fiend from the pit was in pursuit. His shrieks and oaths chased them into the night.

Jack unsteadily got to his feet, bent over with his hands on his knees, then leaned against a wall as a wave of dizziness and nausea swept over him. Juan Gaskara sheathed his sword and returned to Jack. He guided Jack up the ratlines and into one of the chairs by the table. Jack slumped forward, holding his head in his hands. Then the old man locked and bolted the door.

Jack dropped his hands and watched Gaskara. There was no light except for the flickering fire in the grate. He was gasping for breath; the paroxysm that had steeled his muscles was almost past. The remarkable transformation Jack saw, or thought he saw, was gone. Gaskara fumbled for matches, while the eerie bird mumbled and chattered and clacked.

The flickering flames died down. Juan Gaskara's knees were beginning to totter with weakness. He struck a match and lighted a second lamp. Little by little the wick blazed up. Without looking at Jack, Gaskara unbuckled his sword and reprimed the clumsy pistols.

The murderous gleam had almost faded from his eyes, leaving them glossy and lusterless. Dipping an old quill pen in a horn inkstand, he began to write, or, rather, to draw, slowly and laboriously:

His fingers worked quicker after a time. He blotted the paper and looked round.

Jack took a deep breath and sat back in the chair, dropping his hands to his sides. The old man looked at him, and his eyes grew stony with horror. They were fixed rigidly on the mark scrawled on Jack's forehead.

"The mark, the mark!" he gasped.

Juan Gaskara tottered up, one skinny hand clutching his yellow throat, the other clawing the air.

"The mark, the mark," he panted, hoarsely.

His face turned black and hideous. He seemed to be strangling. He fell back over the chair with a crash, and the parrot burst into a peal of hideous laughter.

A dull, reverberating thud shook the door and echoed through the room, sounding like somebody knocking on the lid of a coffin.

CHAPTER SIX

The sullen, reverberating knock was repeated. The sound rang like a hammer-blow through Jack's aching, throbbing head. He managed to rise, but he was so weak that his limbs trembled under him. He caught a glimpse of himself in the wavy glass of a dirty mirror and noticed the mark on the forehead. He grabbed the stained towel hanging next to the mirror, and scrubbed off the mark.

The knock came a third time. Down hopped the parrot from the little carronade, and began to scrape its beak on the rug. It found the paper on which Juan Gaskara had scrawled the hieroglyphics. Seizing it, the bird flapped back to its perch and thrust the paper into the nozzle of the gun.

"Open the door, mate," said a voice. "It is a friend. I want to save you. Ach, do not be afraid."

The tones were as sweet as honey. Jack was too dazed to actually know what he was doing. He staggered to the door and drew back the bolts. A sudden dread made him try to rectify his error. He was not in time. A force more powerful than his own pushed him away and a man entered.

Jack's fear vanished. There was nothing in the appearance of the stranger to excite alarm. But for some reason, the lack of fear was, in itself, disquieting. He was like a stray cat that wanted to approach a friendly person in trust, while simultaneously wanting to run away in fear.

The visitor was short and stout, and his long gray beard lent him quite a paternal air. He was dressed in black, and wore a pair of gold-rimmed spectacles.

"Don't be afraid, young man," he cooed in silky tones. "I am a friend. Fasten the door. Ach, I am a good friend. I wish you no harm."

The voice had an accent that Jack thought came from a country on the Continent. It caused him no uneasiness, so Jack obeyed and bolted the door.

"Why have you come here, and what do you want?" asked Jack. He leaned against the door, trying to disguise how weak he actually felt.

"In good time, mate, in good time," said the man smoothly. "Phew! I got winded climbing the ratlines. I am so fat. Do not be afraid. I wish you no harm."

Jack was starting to get suspicious, as if he was a chubby pig being sized up by a drooling wolf. "You have already said that."

The man smiled in response. He waved toward the unconscious form on the floor. "What happened to Black Juan?"

"I think he is in a fit," answered Jack.

"Well, let him lie there. Young man, I come to do you good. I am Hans Vanderlet, and mine trade is to keep a public-house in Amsterdam. None sells better schnapps than old Hans."

Vanderlet. Jack recognized the name. The same name was mentioned in the bloody tale he read last night, and the same one Gaskara shouted out in his delirium.

Vanderlet stepped closer. Jack instinctively pushed himself away from the door and moved next to the pistols, placing his hand on one. Vanderlet noticed, smiled, held up one hand and stepped back.

"You should not be afraid, but I am very frightened," Vanderlet continued, almost as if telling a bedtime story. "Long ago, Black Juan kill my grandfather. I care not about that, for my heart is tender and kind. I do not wish revenge at all. I sell schnapps, and I wish nothing more but to sell schnapps. Then comes scoundrels to mine house, Swayne, and Lake, and the Honorable, and the Frenchman. They say, 'we've found Black Juan Gaskara who murder your father and our fathers.' They say 'When we have the secret of the treasure he hide, and then we kill him.' I hold up mine hand in horror, for I want not to leave mine home and wife, but only to sell schnapps. But go I must, for my life, or they will kill me. Young man, I warn you to have nothing to do with Black Juan. If you have the accursed secret, give it up and fly, for they will kill you."

"I appreciate your concern about my health, particularly after the incidents of the past two nights." Jack didn't try to hide the sarcasm. "One of them tried to strangle me tonight, and last night another sought to impale me with a knife."

Vanderlet smiled. "Ah, Lake. He is expert with the knife. He can throw a knife from Dusseldorf and hit you. He miss on purpose."

"If that is supposed to be strangely comforting, it is not," Jack said. "However, I have no secret. I don't know what you are talking about."

Vanderlet stroked his beard and shook his head. He went on gently. "It is like this, I am a man of peace. I will be plain with you. There is much treasure, millions in gold and jewels, on Peril Island. Black Juan hide it there. I care not for treasure, but other men love it and worship it. We know not where Peril Island is, or where on it Black Juan conceal the wealth. It is that we want, the location. If you have it, give it up. I wish you no harm, but the rest, they will murder you."

So Black Juan's wild story must be true, Jack thought. If it were a myth, why did these five strange men pursue the old sailor so relentlessly? Jack's brain was clearer, his voice steadier.

"So am I to look upon you as an ambassador?" he asked.

"That is right, that is right," grinned Hans Vanderlet in approval, his hands spread wide. "I come with an ultimatum. No, no, that is the wrong word. What do I wish to say is ... ah ... a proposal. Yes, I come with a proposal. I not want bloodshed, ach, no. I come, too, with money. Leave this place and swear not to see Black Juan no more, and we will give you one hundred pounds."

Vanderlet brought out a greasy purse and poured the coins into his hand. He held them up and shook them, the clinking they made sounding sweet and alluring. "There it be. Take it. Take it ... and be wise."

"Wait," said Jack, "I don't understand yet. The scoundrels almost killed me."

"Yes, they are terrible scoundrels, terrible, terrible men," agreed Vanderlet. "I would give much to get away from them. The money I offer is mine own. I do not wish to see you dead. So simple. Take it. Take the money and leave."

He counted out the coins, carefully placing them on the table in a neat stack. It was the most money Jack had ever laid eyes on.

Jack stared at the speaker. To bribe him so richly for abandoning Juan Gaskara was an ample proof that these men were playing for big stakes, certainly more than a mere one hundred pounds. "What is your object?"

"To get the treasure. I do not lie."

"And what will you do to that man?" Jack pointed to Gaskara.

"They will not hurt him if I can stop them," said Vanderlet, stroking his beard again. "Bah, they care not for him, but only for the wealth. They take the secret and then leave him. Black Juan needs not your pity. No wickeder scoundrel ever live."

Jack hesitated. Things were not adding up. Giving up a man to certain death for one hundred pounds, even one who lived as evilly as Gaskara, smacked distastefully of blood money, and placed Jack in the same league as these blackguards. And, despite Vanderlet's soothing words, there was no guarantee the villains wouldn't slit Jack's throat as soon as he left the room and take the money back. The knife attack strengthened that last possibility. He needed to play for time. "Let me have until morning to decide."

Vanderlet thought for a moment, then nodded. "You shall. I will come in the morning. I do not wish you to die. You are so young, so much to live for. I go now. Old Hans is honest and has a tender heart. There is no treachery in old Hans. No one is hiding outside. Good-night, good-night."

Jack, pistol in hand, opened the door for him. Vanderlet went puffing down the ratlines into the darkness below. Jack shot the bolts, and glanced at the table. Vanderlet had not omitted to take the money with him. But there was a mark on the table that Jack had not noticed before: two circles had been chalked on the green cloth and a cross in the center of the double ring.

Jack grabbed the towel and erased the chalked mark. He glanced at Gaskara, still on the floor. Jack righted the chair, awkwardly picked up Black Juan and placed him in the chair.

Slumping into the other chair, Jack stared at the old man. He felt like he was sitting up with a relative in a sick room. He dozed off.

"Wake up, lad, wake up! Swallow this."

Juan Gaskara was shaking Jack. Some liquid that burnt like scalding water trickled down Jack's throat. He coughed and gagged.

"Have I been sleeping?" he asked.

"Aye, lad, most like. Pull yourself together, for I need a messmate to stand by while I founder. Can ye stand?"

"Yes."

"Take me in tow and put me in that chair."

Jack helped him with difficulty. Gaskara was gray to the lips. He sat with his back to the door. His voice was but a gasp.

"Give me the sword, lad."

Jack did so.

"Hark well, Dick Drayton's grandson," he said. "Ye've stood gallantly by a sinking hulk. 'Tis no use working the pumps now, for Black Juan is sinking. The rum, lad, the rum!"

"I'll get a doctor."

"No doctor for me," the old man ordered. "The rum."

He moistened his ashen lips. Jack poured a glass of rum from the bottle. He handed it to Gaskara. He downed the glass in one gulp, then grabbed Jack's hand with a surprisingly strong grip. His voice was weak, but intense. "Do ye believe in the Almighty, lad?"

"Yes."

"Then ye know my fate. Hellfire and brimstone for eternity because of my wicked deeds. Hark'ee well, Drayton. I've waded in blood for wealth that I ne'er touched. That wealth lies safe in Peril Island." Gaskara broke into a fit of coughing. When he stopped, his voice was a whisper. "I like ye, lad. Ye showed courage and loyalty. When I'm gone push your fist into the old shark's mouth and ye'll find a thousand guineas. Take them, lad, and spend 'em in chartering a boat. Tis little enough, but if ye have a true friend who will aid ye, he may share the secret. The treasure will bring no curse upon ye, lad, if ye but use it for good. And maybe — by the Almighty's mercy and grace — using it for good will wash a spot of sin off my immortal soul."

Gaskara grabbed the front of Jack's shirt. "But beware of the Honorable and Monkey Swayne, and beware of that smooth-tongued villain Vanderlet. The paper is in the handle of the pistol with — with —"

Gaskara broke into another fit of coughing.

"I must get a doctor," Jack said.

"No! Stand by," panted Juan Gaskara. "Get the paper safe and guard it with your life." He gestured at one of the pistols. "Twist the ring to the left."

Jack took the huge flintlock and turned the ring screwed into the handle. A piece of hinged wood shot open. Concealed in the cavity were two rolls of yellow parchment.

"I can't see ye. Have ye found it?"

"Yes sir," answered Jack.

"There are two," the pirate's voice was now just a whisper. "Keep the one with the red cross on it. That's the true one. Make sure."

Jack checked the parchments. "I have it."

"Now slip the other into my pocket for the dogs to find, ha, ha, ha! They'll sail wide of Peril Island if they follow that. Ye'll find my will in among the guineas — More rum, lad, more rum."

Gaskara was dying. Jack refilled the glass. Gaskara drank, placed the glass on the table with a thunk, and closed his eyes.

"I'm getting a doctor," Jack said, slipping the parchment into his inside coat pocket. Locking the door behind him he dashed down the ratlines and out into the narrow street. He almost collided with a policeman.

"I need a doctor," he blurted out. "Where can I find one?"

"In Pedland Street — that's the nearest. Turn sharp on the left, and on the left twice. You'll see the lamp."

Jack raced through the streets and found the house. It was a wretched house and spoke of a miserable and perhaps not too honest practice. He tugged at the night-bell. At last a window upstairs opened and a man's head popped out.

"What do you want?"

"A man is dying," said Jack. "Please make haste —"

"Where?" came the bored question.

"Just off Crosskeys Lane."

"Ten shillings is what I charge. Have you the money to pay in advance?"

"No," said Jack, "but you'll be paid. He's dying —"

"Go somewhere else," interrupted the doctor, and the window closed.

Jack could have killed the man. He tore at the bell, but there was no answer. Then he began to kick and hammer at the door. The doctor refused to appear. Jack ran back to Crosskeys Lane. He plunged into the archway, checked himself with a cry, and recoiled.

At his feet lay the policeman. His helmet had been knocked off and his closely cropped hair was dabbed with blood. Jack sprang over the constable's body. Shrieks and oaths broke the silence. Dark figures were dancing and gesticulating round the foot of the ratlines.

And Black Juan had revived.

"Have at ye, dogs, have at ye," came his shrill cry.

Jack had no weapons. He seized the policeman's whistle and began to blow with all his might. Then came a blaze of red and loud report. A bullet whizzed past his ear.

"Gag the old man," screamed the voice of Monkey Swayne. "Burn you, shoot again, Honorable."

Jack threw himself down. Another tongue of flame leaped out of the darkness, another bullet whistled overhead. Jack got back to his feet, then a hand seized his throat.

"I said I would wait until morning," came the soft voice of Vanderlet from behind Jack. He had a grasp of iron. For the third time a shot startled the echoes. Juan Gaskara threw up his arms and fell.

"Burn you, you've killed him," gasped Monkey Swayne.

"He's merely stabbed," replied the Honorable. "Search him, quick."

"Got it, I've got it!" Monkey Swayne brandished a roll of parchment. Police whistles shattered the night. "Run, run! The police, the police!"

"We have no need of you. You should have taken my generous offer." Vanderlet released Jack.

Jack turned toward Vanderlet, just in time to see him bring down the butt of a gun square on his head. A blaze of sparks danced in his eyes. Jack stumbled a few steps and lay motionless across the body of Juan Gaskara.

CHAPTER SEVEN

Jack was lying in one of the white cots in the hospital, muttering and drifting between an out-of-focus world and a dark one. After a time, he didn't know for how long, the mist started to clear, and he began to see and understand. He grew aware of a red-faced doctor and pretty nurse frequently standing by his bed, always seemingly saying the same thing.

"Don't you think he's strong enough, Doctor Drew?" the nurse would ask.

"In another day or two nurse, in another day or two," the doctor would answer.

Jack wondered why that they could not find some other thing to say.

Little by little the fog lifted. One morning he awoke and his head seemed clearer. He was the only occupant of one of four cots stuffed into a small room, along with a tiny table and a single chair. It appeared as if a former storage room had been turned into some type of overflow ward. He heard voices on the other side of the door to his room.

"Going to turn his toes up, eh?" inquired one voice.

"Not this trip, Inspector. He's just come round." Jack recognized the doctor's voice.

"I'll have a look at him, then."

Jack propped himself up by pillows. In walked the doctor and a rumbled-looking man.

"Well, my lad," said the man kindly, as if addressing a small, but not particularly bright, child, "I'm Inspector Tasker. You're awake, are you? Good. Got anything to say, any statement to make? It doesn't matter if you don't feel well enough. Try and remember now. Can you talk?"

"I was not born dumb," Jack said.

"Oh, I am glad to hear that. Don't go, doctor. Chirp away, my lad."

Jack smiled faintly. "You are rather familiar, considering our short acquaintance," he said, and his refined voice made both doctor and Inspector stare at him with renewed curiosity, "but I'm not particular."

"A gentleman, by jingo!" muttered the police officer. He asked aloud, "What's your name, sir?"

"Jack Drayton. Present address, a barge anchored a few rods above Lucknan's Wharf. Income, nil; prospects uncertain. Is there anything else?"

Both the listeners laughed as Jack jerked out this information.

"You're a good plucked one," said the Inspector. "Now, what about this affair?"

"Is the old man dead?"

"He shot himself."

Jack clenched his hands. "A lie," he cried. "Juan Gaskara was murdered. I know the man who killed him."

"What?" gasped the doctor.

The Inspector winked at the doctor and bent toward him. He whispered with the medico for a moment, and the medico nodded. "And who was the man, then, Mr. Drayton?"

"I don't know his name. He is described as the 'Honorable.' I could identify him anywhere. He shot at me when I was trying to rescue the old man. His accomplices were Swayne, Lake, Guerin, and Vanderlet."

"Who's that — the last one?" the Inspector sputtered.

"Vanderlet — Hans Vanderlet."

"What did I tell you, doctor?" said the Inspector, in an undertone. "It's no use bothering. Vanderlet is a gent with plenty of money, and is highly respected. This poor chap has been knocked about the head too much."

"Yes; that's it," agreed the doctor. "He will be better later on."

They left the room, leaving Jack to seethe in anger at the Inspector's attitude.

Gaskara was dead. He had died a death of violence — such a death as he had dealt out to many. It was retribution long delayed. But the horror of the night had not lifted its shadow. Jack could see the dent hacked in Juan Gaskara's door, see the blood-stained, whirling sword, hear the phantom shrieks and the sullen splashing of phantom corpses. It had only been a nightmare, it must have been, an evil dream, but it was all so hideously vivid.

He heard two voices outside his room. One belonged to the Inspector, the other one sounded familiar, although Jack couldn't place it immediately.

"I can't make it out," said the Inspector.

"It was remarkable. The poor young man seemed touched," cooed the second one.

"Wrong in the head, eh?"

"Yes, yes. He not quite fainted when I run up. He say three or four men attack him, but it was not so, for I see it all. It very sad. Poor fellow, poor fellow."

Jack sat bolt upright in his bed. He knew the second voice: Vanderlet.

"Oh, he's sure to ramble then," said the Inspector. "We know where to find you, sir. Good morning."

Jack grew hot with rage. He wanted to give that stupid Inspector what for. He flung off the covers and got up. The room spun nauseatingly. Jack sprawled back into bed, trying to calm down.

Vanderlet had practically silenced him. At the very least, he had fixed it so that nobody — including the police — would credit Jack's story about the murder of Black Juan Gaskara, a freebooter of eighty years ago. The tale was too wildly impossible. It would be risking a madhouse to tell that tale in court. There would be an inquest, about nine-days' sensation in the press, and then all would be forgotten.

The door opened and the nurse came in. Her red hair blazed against her starched cap. She looked at Jack and folded her arms.

"What's all this, then?" she asked. "Trying to get out of bed, are we?"

Jack mumbled a non-answer and tried to pull up the covers. The nurse came over, professionally and efficiently tucking him in. Jack got an intoxicating whiff of the lavender scent she wore.

"The inspector thinks you're balmy on the crumpet," she said, nodding toward the hallway.

"Do you?"

The nurse stopped fiddling and fixed a gaze on Jack with her bright blue eyes. After a second examination, she smiled and shook her head.

"Thank you, sister ... ?"

"That is an old-fashioned term, isn't it? I am not a nun.

I prefer to be addressed as 'nurse.' Nurse Soames," she answered formally. Then she picked up the tray holding the glass and water pitcher and leaned in slightly. "Agnes."

Jack smiled. "Thank you, Nurse Agnes Soames."

She returned the smile. "I better not hop the wag. I will check back later, Mr. —"

"Jack. I prefer to be addressed as Jack. I shall look forward to you checking back."

"Jack." She seemed to try the name on for size. "Me too. Ta."

She glided out of the room like a shadow.

Agnes returned several times that day, seeming to Jack more often than it appeared necessary to complete the needed tasks. These visits only lasted for a few minutes at a time, but the two filled the brief periods with conversation and laughter. Jack wished her stays could be longer.

In the early afternoon the following day, there was a soft knock on the door. Agnes poked her head in.

"Oh, good. You're awake. There's a gentleman here to see you," she said.

"Inspector balmy on the crumpet?"

Agnes laughed. "No, your brother."

"My brother?"

Hector pushed his way into the room. "This is a fine how-de-do! You leave me on that dingy barge while you rest here between crisp, clean white sheets."

Agnes confronted Hector. "He has concussion."

"Ha! Likely story," Hector plopped himself down on the chair, draping one arm over the back. He patted his stomach. "Dyspepsia, more like it."

Agnes moved toward Jack. "Would you like me to get the doctor, Jack?"

Hector cocked an eyebrow. "'Jack,' is it?"

"No, thank you, Agnes, it's fine. He is impossible sometimes, but he's really a brick," Jack shot a dirty look toward Hector, "most of the time."

Hector nodded in appreciation.

"If you say so. I'll check back later. When you're alone," Agnes added pointedly.

Jack smiled a response. Agnes returned the smile and left the room, closing the door.

"I brought your book of sonnets to keep you occupied during your lonely convalescence." Hector held it up and glanced toward the door. "I see I needn't have bothered."

"Shut up and give it here." Jack caught the tossed book. "My brother?"

"It was the only way I was sure to get in. I must say that you are looking fine, concussion or no. I should be cross with you, old chap. You just left me in the lurch and disappeared one night. You said you would only be gone for a few hours. And that I worry like an old woman, as a topper. Now don't try to deny it, that is exactly what you said. I have been searching for you high and low. When I read in the paper about an incident with old man dressed from the last century, I figured that must have been that Gaskara fellow. The story related that when the old man had attacked a constable, an unidentified stranger — you, I presumed — tried to intervene, and got clonked on the head for your trouble. Then Gaskara blew out his brains rather than be captured. I traced you to this hospital."

Jack shook his head. "It was not suicide."

"That's what it said in the papers."

"It was murder."

Hector sat up straight in the chair. "Murder! Did you tell the police?"

"I did. The inspector did not believe me. Knocked about in the head too much, don't you know." Jack tapped one finger to his temple and sighed. "Gaskara's dead. Those fiends will run for it, and Gaskara deserved all. Why should I speak?"

He thought for a moment. "But am I doing right in permitting Juan Gaskara's murderers to escape? Surely, if ever a man deserved a swift, violent death, it was that pirate. And vengeance came fitly from the hand of the grandson of one of his victims. I don't know. I hope the last chapter of this vile story of blood and crime is written," muttered Jack. "Let the dead sleep."

"Perhaps that's true. The revels now have ended, and these are actors as I have foretold you," Hector stood up and went to the door. "Now that I know where you are, and that you are being properly attended to, I'll pop back tomorrow. By the way, I find sonnet number 18 particularly good for romance."

Hector ducked the thrown pillow as he darted out the door. Jack retrieved his pillow, punched and fluffed it a few times in an attempt to make it comfortable. He propped himself up and opened the book with a contented sigh.

Agnes returned a little later, carrying an armload of linen. She started changing the bedding of one of the cots, although it probably didn't need it. She nodded toward the book.

"Did your brother bring you that?"

Jack laughed. "He is my closest friend, but not my brother."

"I didn't think so. You two don't resemble each other at all."

Jack held up his book. "Do you read much, Agnes?"

"Only medical journals."

"Medical journals?"

"I want to be a doctor," she said crisply, but adamantly. She faced Jack and stood up straight, as though expecting an argument.

Jack's impression of Agnes was that she was the type of person who got what she aimed for. He wondered if he was in her sights. He hoped so. "I have absolutely no doubt you will achieve exactly that."

Agnes relaxed and smiled, then returned to her task.

"But medical journals are so dry." Jack opened his book, and flipped through some pages. He stopped on one. "Here, listen to this:

> *Shall I compare thee to a summer's day?*
> *Thou art more lovely and more temperate:*
> *Rough winds do shake the darling buds of May,*
> *And summer's lease hath all too short a date:*
> *Sometime too hot the eye of heaven shines,*
> *And often is his gold complexion dimm'd;*
> *And every fair from fair sometime declines,*
> *By chance, or nature's changing course, untrimm'd;*
> *But thy eternal summer shall not fade*
> *Nor lose possession of that fair thou ow'st;*
> *Nor shall Death brag thou wander'st in his shade,*
> *When in eternal lines to time thou grow'st;*
> *So long as men can breathe or eyes can see,*
> *So long lives this, and this gives life to thee."*

"That's beautiful," Agnes said softly. "What's it called?"

"It is Shakespeare's sonnet number 18," Jack answered. He closed the book, held it out and smiled. "Here. Something to read between those journal articles."

"Oh, I couldn't take a ..."

"Consider it only a loan, then. Return it when you finish with it."

"Thank you." Agnes took the book and glanced through the pages.

A loud voice came from the other side of the door. "I believe Sister Soames is with that gentleman patient — again."

"Oh, I may be in trouble," Agnes said quickly as she slipped the book into the pocket of her apron. She gathered up the dirty linen and left.

The next morning, Agnes ushered a stranger, dressed in a stylish frock coat and gold-rimmed eyeglasses, into the room. She seemed very excited about something, but stepped out of the room before Jack could ask why.

"Mr. Drayton," said the stranger, "my name is Mr. Halliday."

"Pleased to meet you, sir," replied the bewildered Jack.

"I think this meeting will be very pleasant for both of us," said Mr. Halliday. "I represent your uncle —"

"Kindly inform my uncle that I have no —"

Mr. Halliday held up a hand to interrupt Jack. "Please, Mr. Drayton, please! Allow me to continue! I am well aware of your relationship with your uncle."

Jack nodded a curt apology.

"I represent your uncle's estate."

"Estate?"

"Your uncle died a month ago."

"Oh." Jack thought he should feel something, but didn't.

"He left everything to you in his will."

"He did?" Jack asked in a surprised voice.

"Yes, he did," Mr. Halliday confirmed. "That includes his London townhouse, its contents and an income of approximately £14500 a year. I heartily congratulate you, sir."

Jack was in stunned silence for a moment. He finally stammered out "How did you find me?"

"Through the doctor. We advertised in the *Times*, and the doctor saw the notice. He wrote to us at once. The will gave me some authority, so I kept Mrs. Clare on as the housekeeper and cook. I hope you do not mind."

Jack grinned. "Mrs. Clare! No, of course not! She was more than a mother to me when I lived with my uncle."

The doctor and Agnes were now standing in the door. Both were smiling.

Jack found himself laughing foolishly. He climbed out of bed a little unsteadily, then shook hands with Mr. Halliday, and the doctor. When he reached Agnes, they held hands for a moment, then embraced.

The next day Jack and Agnes stepped out of the hospital into its dingy courtyard. Even though the sun was shining overhead, the gray walls seemed to suck in all the light, shrouding the courtyard in perpetual gloom. Despite that, Jack felt wonderful being outside again. He shyly took Agnes' hand. She looked into his eyes, smiled, and tightened the grip. They started to stroll around the courtyard.

"I still have trouble believing it," Jack said. "Fortune's wheel has turned swiftly. I had been clinging to its bottom like grim death, dreading to lose my grip on the slippery spokes. Now I'm heading for the top, more certain and secure than I have been in years." He grinned and shook his head. "It is like a Dickens novel, maybe *Little Doritt*. A pauper unexpectedly inherits wealth from an uncle. I always thought those twists were unlikely plot contrivances and often found them amusing. Now I'm living it."

They stopped by a worn-out bench. The gnarled stump behind it indicated that a tree had shaded it at one time. They sat, laughing as the bench wobbled alarmingly. They were quiet for a moment, Jack simply enjoying being in Agnes' company.

"You seemed happy ..." Agnes started. She stopped and looked away.

"What? What were you about to say?"

Agnes shook her head. "Nothing."

"Oh, come on," Jack playfully nudged her and grinned. "What were you going to say?"

Agnes met his eyes. "You seemed ... forgive me ... but you seemed happy that your uncle died."

"Yes, yes, it did appear that way," he said quietly. He shifted his gaze to the ground, ashamed.

"Weren't you fond of your uncle?"

Jack shook his head. "No. We didn't get along. We were like chalk and cheese. He was my father's older brother, a life-long bachelor. I don't think he even liked children."

"He took care of you."

Jack leaned back on the bench and stared into the gray sky. "Yes, he did, and probably he didn't have to. When my parents died, I could have easily been packed off to an orphanage. Oh, I'm positive my uncle would have sent some extra shillings each month to make sure I was treated well."

"But he didn't pack you off, did he."

"I think he believed having me in an orphanage would besmirch the family name."

"That's mean, Jack."

"No, no he didn't pack me off when he could have." Jack bit off the words. His insides were churning from this talk about his uncle. He stood. "I wonder why this tree was cut down."

"Did he try?"

"Maybe the tree was diseased. That's funny, isn't it?" Jack forced a toneless laugh. "A diseased tree at a hospital. You would think they could cure it."

"Did you try, Jack?'

"They should plant another one, but there doesn't seem to be much sunlight —"

"Did you and your uncle try?"

"You certainly do ask a lot of questions, Nurse Soames." Jack tried to laugh. It was a feeble joke, and it was met by dead silence. He went on irritably. "Did he and I try what?"

"Did you two try to get along with each other?"

"No! Yes! I don't know!" Jack exploded.

Agnes' blue eyes seemed to peer deep into him, peeling back his soul in layers like an onion. "I don't want to talk about him. Please," he pleaded softly. He turned on his heel. "I think it is time to go back inside."

Jack took a couple of steps and halted. He still felt Agnes' eyes on him, sad and disappointed. "It's time to stop running, Jack," he said in a low voice. "It's time to stop running."

He meekly returned to the bench and sat. He leaned forward, cradling his head in his hands.

"My uncle and I were like neighboring countries living in a constant state of undeclared war, with border skirmishes frequently breaking out," he said after a long pause to find the right words, "and no peace talks scheduled."

Jack slumped back on the bench. He stared vacantly ahead.

"I was angry, so very, very angry," Jack said with a tired voice. "I was angry at the unfairness of my parent's death. I was angry at my uncle taking their spot. I was angry that my uncle couldn't take their spot. I was angry at the whole, wide world."

Jack leaned his head on Agnes' soft shoulder. She stroked his hair.

The doctor released Jack from the hospital a day later. He thanked the doctor, and then asked Agnes if they could meet again. When she said yes, he left the hospital feeling that getting a concussion had some benefits after all.

He may have inherited some money, but he had none of it in his pocket now, so he headed toward the wharves on foot. He turned into a square after walking a while. A few smoky, unhealthy trees were scattered about with seats under them. Glad to rest his limbs, he sat down.

I wonder if any human being ever had such a blood-curdling experience? Jack thought. He let out a long breath. *I must let it drop. If I begin to spin that yarn in a court of law, to the asylum I should go in two shakes of a lamb's tale. Poor old Gaskara!*

He began to think what he should have done, what he could have done to help Gaskara. He reviewed what he should have said, how to have taken him to help, and what other things he could have tried. Finally, how he had failed him.

Another thought glided into Jack's mind, like a train switching to another track. Why was he not thinking about his "poor old uncle"? He heard Agnes ask her question again: did he try to get along with his uncle? He must have, surely. He searched his memory, but he couldn't think of one single example.

That made him uncomfortable, so Jack stood and continued on his journey, trying to focus on the future. He finally reached the docks. He knew that he was moving away from the area, and noticed, as if for the first time, how run down it was, how dirty it was, how much poverty there was.

"Goodbye to the East-end, and good riddance," Jack growled.

Instantly, he realized how wrong he was. The East-end had given him shelter, and its hospital had taken him in. As Marsden rowed to pick him up, Jack understood that there were good, along with the not-so-good, people living here. He made up his mind that he would do his utmost to make the area a better place.

He exchanged greetings with Marsden as he climbed into the boat.

"I haven't seen you for a while. Where have you been keeping yourself?" Marsden asked.

"I've been in hospital," Jack answered.

"Hospital! Anything serious?"

Jack smiled. "No. Just a bump on the head. My least vulnerable spot."

As they reached the barge, Jack spotted Hector doing exercises on deck.

"Ahoy, *Etruria*!" hailed Jack. "Prepare to be boarded!"

Hector sauntered over to the railing and leaned on it. "Jack, my boy! It's about time you returned! What did Agnes do? Finally throw you out?"

Jack climbed on deck. "Yes. She couldn't stand another visit from you."

"Ha! You're just jealous!" Hector shook Jack's hand. "Welcome back, old chap."

"Thanks." Jack leaned over the railing to Marsden. "You don't mind waiting, do you Marsden?"

"Not a bit."

"Thanks. I just have to change." Jack turned to Hector. "Come with me. I have something to tell you."

Jack and Hector went to the cabin. As Jack changed into his better suit, he filled Hector in on his uncle's death and his inheritance.

"That is something," Hector said, "although I don't know whether to congratulate you or give my condolences."

"Either one or both," Jack replied as he fixed his tie, watching himself in the small, cracked mirror. He stopped as an idea occurred to him. "I guess I'm the last living member of my family now."

"You have my condolences on your uncle's passing and congratulations on the inheritance," Hector said. "What do you plan to do with the *Etruria*?"

Jack patted the cabin's wall and smiled. "I've grown rather fond of the old girl. I think I'll keep her and fix her up. I'll take her sailing on the Thames, once I learn how. Maybe I'll name you her captain."

Hector chuckled.

"I have to see the solicitor, Mr. Halliday, today — for the official reading of the will and all that, I suppose — and then possibly the banker." Jack faced Hector. "Hector, I'm still a bit overwhelmed and shaky by all of this news. I hate to ask you to sit through boring meetings that have nothing to do with you, but I could certainly use a friend at hand to keep me on an even keel."

"No need to apologize!" Hector grinned as he brushed some lint off of Jack's shoulders. "Of course, I'd be honored and delighted to be your second. Let me change into something more presentable."

Marsden rowed them to the landing, with Hector paying for both trips. They strolled to Mr. Halliday's office. The sun was shining, the air was warm and sweet. Jack enjoyed the walk, instead of dreading it because he was broke and had no other means of transport. It took a few hours sitting in a stuffy office for Jack to sign papers, go through the household inventory, and finally receive the keys. Mr. Halliday then escorted them to meet the banker who handled all his uncle's — now his — investments. They left the bank, some of Jack's inheritance fattening his billfold.

"Now, to buy you a good meal," Jack announced as he pointed to a restaurant across the street, "to repay you for some of what you spent on me."

"I certainly won't say no to that," Hector said, "but there's a better restaurant just around the corner."

"How do you know that?"

"Oh, that's what I heard," Hector shrugged off and guided Jack down another street. Hector ordered a delicious meal for them both, as though he knew his way around the menu of fancy restaurants, then persuaded Jack to detour to a shop on Regent Street to buy new clothes which were, as Hector put it, "more in keeping with Jack's new station."

It was early evening by the time they stood on the stoop of the townhouse, located on a quiet, tree-lined street fronting a large square. The keys dangled from Jack's hand, his new, rather conservative dark suit contrasting with Hector's new sporty striped one. Under Jack's arm was a box containing his old clothes. They stood in front of the shiny black front door for a long time.

"Well, what are you waiting for?" prodded Hector.

"When I left, I swore that I would never ..." Jack said quietly. "I was ten when my parents died and my uncle took me in. It was his duty, he said. A fact he reminded me of almost every day. It was his duty."

He was silent for a moment, then looked at Hector. "You asked some good questions this afternoon at Mr. Halliday's office, and at the bank. It made me realize that, even after knowing you these past two years, I know nothing about your background or your upbringing. You never talk about your family."

"That is correct. I do not."

Full stop.

"That is it, then?" Jack asked.

"That is it."

"For all I know," Jack went on, exasperated at Hector's reticence, "you could be the wayward prince nobody in the royal family discusses in polite company."

"A baronet, actually," Hector corrected. He nodded toward the door. "Are you going to open that door, or do we stand out here all night?"

Jack grumbled a response, then inserted the key into the lock and turned it. Even after over two years, the clunk of the lock sounded familiar ... and repressive. Jack swung the heavy door open. He and Hector stepped into the entrance hall.

It was just as he remembered it: the polished wood floors, the carpeted staircase rising at the far end of the hall, two wood-paneled doors on the right wall. The two large landscape paintings on the left wall, flanking the grandfather clock. The clock's sonorous ticking just seemed to make the house emptier. Memories struck Jack like a physical force.

"It happened right here, right here in this hallway." Jack saw the scene replayed as if he was watching it enacted on the stage. "My uncle and I engaged in our loudest, biggest, most vicious argument we ever had. We were like two tomcats fighting in a back alley. We had been at each other all day. One argument after another argument after another argument. Mostly over trivial, silly things. Funny, the arguments always seemed to be over unimportant items that grew so important in the moment. Almost as if the actual fights themselves were of more import than what we were fighting about. The battles that day kept building and building, hour after hour. Suddenly, I just had it. I just had my fill. I ended the whole thing by walking out that door and giving it a good slam. I spent a cold night in the park, promising myself never to return, then signed on as a deck steward the next morning. My last memory of my uncle is his rage, red in the face, shaking his fist. Now there is no hope of an apology, no hope of reconciliation, for either of us."

Hector put a hand on Jack's shoulder. "Are you feeling all right?"

Jack started a little at Hector's touch. He forced a smile. "Yes. Well, how about a grand tour?"

Hector nodded and patted Jack on the back. "Of course. Lead on!"

Jack put down the box he was holding, and speaking like a tour guide at a great country house, he went to the first door.

"Our first stop will be the library." He opened the door and gestured for Hector to go in.

The library wasn't a large room, but every available inch of wall space was occupied with books. A few piles of volumes which wouldn't fit in the bookcases stood stacked by the front window. The warm, comforting smell of leather-bound volumes filled the room.

"This is wizard!" Hector walked the perimeter of the room, running his fingers along the book spines. "I could spend hours in here."

Jack nodded. "I did. The library is my favorite room in the house. I think I have read almost all of these volumes. Fiction, nonfiction, it made no difference. I read them all. Sometimes the library was my refuge, and books were my escape."

"Was it truly as bad as that?" asked Hector.

"It seemed so at the time." Jack was silent for a moment, then he opened a pair of connecting sliding doors. "And now, the parlor."

The two stepped into the parlor, furnished in the high style of the last century, then back into the main hall through the other door.

Jack led Hector to the downstairs hall. "The kitchen is up front. It is definitely Mrs. Clare's domain. She's the housekeeper and cook. Mrs. Clare was the only person my uncle respected ... and I think feared, a little."

They walked toward the back of the house, passing by the box room and ending up in the cozy dining room. They returned to the main hall and climbed the stairs to the second floor, pausing momentarily to admire the garden from the landing window. Jack stopped in the upstairs hall.

"This was my uncle's realm. Bedroom up front, small sitting room here, and the bath."

"So you have indoor plumbing?"

"I do hope you are acquainted with its use."

"I have had some experience."

"I should have left you on the barge."

"But you didn't, gov'ner, bless you," Hector spoke in a Cockney accent as he tapped his straw hat in a two-fingered salute. "So you'll take your uncle's old room?"

Jack shook his head. "No ... no, I couldn't. You take it. After all, you're a baronet, or so you say. Go take a look. I'm going upstairs."

"You're a gentleman and a scholar." Hector grinned and went to explore the suite.

Jack slowly climbed the stairs to the third floor, feeling as if he was stepping back in time. How familiar it all was, and how strange the familiarity seemed. This floor wasn't finely finished as the first two floors; in fact, it was quite plain, and probably originally meant for servants. Three small bedrooms and a bath. He walked to the front bedroom. His old room. He took a deep breath and opened the door.

It was just as he left it that fateful night two years ago. The book he was reading still rested on the nightstand. His schoolbooks haphazardly arranged on the small table. He opened the wardrobe. His clothes were still neatly hanging in place. Everything seemed to await his return, as though he had just stepped out for a moment.

The room was clean, dusted, but otherwise untouched. His uncle hadn't changed a thing.

Jack was shocked. He hadn't expected this. He assumed his uncle would have cleared out the room of his possessions in a fit of pique when he walked out.

Confused, he stepped back and closed the door. His head was in a whirl; too much had happened to him in the past few days for it all to make sense. The grandfather clock downstairs struck the hour, sounding like the toll of a funeral bell.

Ghosts. There were ghosts walking the halls.

CHAPTER EIGHT

"Keep your left up," Hector coached.

Jack and Hector warily circled each other. They had commandeered and cleared out the box room from Mrs. Clare's domain to use for boxing. It was small, but serviceable for sparring.

Hector threw a left, and Jack easily blocked it. Hector nodded in approval. Jack feigned a right cross. When Hector moved to block it, Jack delivered a body blow with his left. Hector staggered backward and held up his hands in surrender.

"You are a good student!" Hector removed his boxing gloves.

"I have a good teacher." Jack also removed his gloves and the two shook hands.

"Mr. Jack," Mrs. Clare stood in the doorway holding the clothing box. She was the picture of the matronly housekeeper, complete with silver-hair and apple checks. She held up a box. "Shall I dispose of your old clothes?"

Earlier that day, Jack had paid a visit to the *Etruria*, packed up his meager belongings and brought them to his new lodgings. He told Marsden of his change of fortune, change of address, then paid him to keep an eye on the barge. Then he visited Agnes at the hospital to ask her to dinner, and happily she accepted.

"No, no, no!" Jack took the box from Mrs. Clare. "These are souvenirs of times past."

"Just as you say, sir," Mrs. Clare said doubtfully.

"Oh, and I will be taking the rear bedroom on the third floor," Jack said.

"You will not be using your old room, Mr. Jack?"

"No ... no."

"I'll see that it is made ready, sir."

"Thank you. You are a wonder, Mrs. Clare!" Jack kissed her on the cheek.

"Oh, Mr. Jack, always the flirt!" Mrs. Clare blushed and headed down the hall to the kitchen.

Jack put the box on the only chair in the room. He opened the box and pulled out his old pea-coat.

"Souvenirs, old chap? This old thing?" Hector came next to Jack. He felt the coat's worn material, shaking his head in disapproval. He stopped. "What's this? Down here? It feels like paper. You weren't reduced to using old newspaper to keep the cold out, were you?"

"No," Jack reached into the coat. He pulled out a roll of parchment that was about nine inches square. It bore signs of age. The corners were stained, and the edges ragged.

"Great goodness!" Hector gasped in wonder. "What's this all about?"

"The doctor told me that the concussion may make my memory of that night a little spotty, but I think Gaskara gave it to me the night he was killed. I think he wanted me to have it."

Jack put the box on the floor and sat in the chair. He spread the parchment out upon his knee. The parchment looked meaningless and absurd. It was covered with drawings in pale, faded ink. They were cleverly executed. More than half the parchment was blank. He turned it over. On the back was written:

"Peril Island,
March 9, 1826,
J. Gaskara."

Hector picked up the parchment and held it closer to the light.

"Peril Island," Jack said to himself. He looked at Hector. "Do you remember that story you read, the one on the linen?"

"Of course. I can't get it out of my mind."

Jack examined the cryptogram minutely. "Peril Island ... that is where Gaskara said he was stranded. I wonder if it is also the island referred to in the linen."

"But Jack," Hector said, "what does it mean?"

Jack tapped the parchment. "This paper could reveal the secret of Black Juan Gaskara's treasure."

"That's unbelievable!" Hector exclaimed. "Have you tried to decipher it?"

"I haven't had the chance. Truth be told, I forgot I had it."

Hector took the parchment. "We're both fond of cryptograms. Baffling as it looks, it can't be that difficult. A half-educated seaman like Juan Gaskara could hardly invent a cipher or series of ciphers that men of brains like us could not discover by patience and diligence!"

"Your modesty is refreshing."

"Besides, this parchment may be sounding the clarion call of adventure, old chap!"

"The clarion call of adventure?" Jack grinned.

"Certainly! Shoveling coal and attending to passengers' dreary wants does not an adventurous life make. Nor does padding around a London townhouse. Allan Quatermain may have had King Solomon's mine, but we have Black Juan Gaskara's treasure! Adventure, dear boy, adventure awaits!" Hector laughed and slapped Jack's shoulder with the back of his hand. "It's a waste of time to examine this wild medley of mystery down here. Let's go up to the library where the light is better. And it is more comfortable."

"Juan gave it to me, and it is supposed to contain a secret. But we still have to read the thing first," Jack pointed out as he followed Hector upstairs.

In the hallway, Jack suddenly stopped and glanced toward the staircase leading to the second floor.

"What's the matter?" asked Hector.

Jack gave an embarrassed laugh. "I half-expected to see my uncle coming down the stairs, ready to argue with me over my inappropriate attire."

"He's gone, Jack," Hector said gently.

"Yes, yes. You are right. He is." Jack took a deep breath and released it, then tapped the parchment in Hector's hand. "Well, let us answer ... what did you call it again?"

Hector grinned. "The clarion call of adventure!"

"Right! The clarion call of adventure! Onward!"

They went into the library. Hector pulled two books off the stack by the window, and used them to hold the parchment open on the table. Then he pulled up a chair and rummaged through the table drawer.

"What are you looking for?" Jack asked.

"Drawing paper and a pen — ha! Here they are!" Hector pulled out a sheet of rough drawing paper and tore it to match the size of the original parchment. Then he picked up the pen.

"What are you doing?"

"I'm making a copy," Hector explained. "Let's not ruin the original by scribbling on it while we're trying to solve the puzzle, shall we? Perhaps you can make yourself useful and find out some more information on Juan Gaskara."

Jack bowed. "Your wish is my command, my liege."

"Stash it."

"Bad-tempered monkey!" Jack laughed and turned toward a bookcase. "I believe there is a copy of Dolland's *Times of the West Indies* around here somewhere. It has a chapter on piracy." He scanned the line of titles. After a few minutes, he pulled out a volume and opened it. He leafed through some pages. "Here it is, old chap. I'll read it. Dolland says: *'The audacity and cruelty of Juan Gaskara are unequaled even in the blood-stained annals of piracy.'*"

"A rather lurid writing style."

"Shut up. To continue:

'He knew no fear; he knew no mercy. His crew consisted of the best fighting men of any age. His men were mostly the scum of British and French warships, born fighters, and well trained, who had fled from justice. No less cruel and blood-thirsty than himself were the desperado's chosen officers — Swayne, Vanderlet, Lake, Guerin, and Santley. Santley was an American and a gentleman born. He had fought under Washington. His barbarous treatment of some British prisoners taken in the war ended in exile. In eight years that ghastly vessel the Satan burned and destroyed eighty-eight ships to human knowledge. How many others that sank riddled by her shot we shall never learn. The treasure gained by Gaskara must have been fabulous. The Satan vanished in the year 1824. It was a most tempestuous year, and it is presumed that the unholy scourge of the seas was lost with all hands in one of the frequent storms.'"

He closed the book and re-shelved it. "There's plenty of fact. A man named Juan Gaskara carried on an extensive and thoroughly illegal business shortly before the date written on the parchment. That's plain history. He, no doubt, accumulated a lot of treasure. All at once he was lost sight of, and it was thought that his vessel had foundered. But that's Dolland's version. It must be the parchment those villains were after. Swayne, Vanderlet, and the rest."

Jack went to the table to check Hector's handiwork. "That's rather good. You would have made an excellent forger."

Hector glanced up from his task. "Maybe I was once. Anyway, almost done. I just need another half hour or so."

"Don't take too long. Remember, we have a dinner engagement with Agnes and her friend she's especially bringing to meet you," Jack went to the door. "I'm going to get ready since I'm not going semi-classical. Oh, and Mrs. Clare leaves for the day in a couple of hours. In case you need her help with your tie."

Jack ducked the flying book.

Jack and Hector spent a wonderful time that night with Agnes, and her friend Elizabeth. They started with dinner, followed by the theater. It was around midnight when Jack and Hector returned home and finally went to bed. Jack dreamed of pirates, savage islands, and vast treasure. He thought the treasure was found. The spade he was digging with struck something with a hollow sound. He scraped away the moist brown earth with feverish hands.

"The treasure, the treasure!" he panted.

He saw the top of a heavy chest. It was strengthened by broad bands of tarnished brass. The lust of gold had seized him. He wanted it all; no one else should touch a single coin. He turned around, fearing that he was being watched. A low, red sun threw a shadow across him. He looked up and saw the evil eyes of Monkey Swayne glaring at him malignantly.

With a cry of terror, Jack awoke. It was no dream. The horrid eyes were glaring at him through the semi-gloom, the twisted, wrinkled, ferret face was close to his. And Swayne's talons closed upon his throat.

Jack struggled with all his might. Swayne knelt on his chest, and a weight fell across Jack's legs. He was choking, stifling.

"Burn me, I'll kill him now!" Swayne pulled out his knife, and poised it to plunge down into Jack's chest.

"Kill him not unless we get the paper," commanded the soft, oily voice of Vanderlet. "The paper we find on Gaskara make no sense. Lake and Guerin do not find anything in his room, only that parrot. The bird fly away. It certainly had no map, so Gaskara must give it to this lad. We may need to force him to tell us where it is. Give him the rag, Honorable."

Something wet and sweet-smelling was pressed over Jack's nose and mouth. His brain reeled, his senses faded.

Sometime later, Jack slowly climbed out of his bed in stages, finally standing upright, although swaying slightly. He looked around his room with the tumbled clothes, the open doors and ransacked drawers. He staggered down to the second floor. He stopped at the base of the stairs.

"Hector?" he called.

A groan answered from farther down the hall. Jack unsteadily made his way toward the sound. He found walking harder than he expected. His legs did not seem to belong to him, and they wanted to make journeys on their own account. His head buzzed. After what seemed like an hour later he finally came upon Hector, sitting in the corner by his bedroom door, cradling his head in his hands.

"Hector?"

Hector looked up with a weak smile. He held out his hands, and Jack pulled him to his feet.

"Jack," he said slowly, "this is a bit too warm. It takes my breath away."

"They nearly took mine. What happened?"

"I was having a lovely dream about the lovely Elizabeth, when I woke up because I thought I heard somebody creeping about the place. I got up to investigate. Somebody pressed something over my face. First thing I knew, I don't know anything."

"Chloroform."

"So that's what chloroform smells like," Hector said. "Did you see who it was?"

"Have a guess."

"Our friends from the barge? Do I win the prize?"

"Exactly right, but no prize. We know the prize they were after," Jack said.

Without saying anything else, they started moving toward the stairs, walking as they used to when their ships were plowing through rough seas. They paused at the top of the stairs for a breath, then made their way to the library. Jack switched on the light. He winced at the glare, and held one hand up to shield his eyes.

"What priced head have you?" Jack muttered. He lowered his hand, and looked at the library table. The items on it had been swept off. The drawer had been pulled out, its contents dumped on the floor. Jack got on his knees and shifted through the mess. There was no parchment. "It's gone."

Hector began to laugh.

"What is so funny?" Jack demanded as he climbed back to his feet. "Has the chloroform turned you into a juggins?"

Hector shook his head and moved to a bookshelf. He pulled out Dolland's *Times of the West Indies,* and opened it to the middle. He pulled out the original parchment.

"The only thing they stole was my copy," Hector said. "I put the copy in the drawer so that the ink would dry. I hoped that if I clamped the actual parchment in a book, it would flatten out the roll, so I put it in Dolland's. It seemed an appropriate place."

"Brilliant!" Jack applauded, then he became more subdued. "I tell you, Hector, old Juan was right when he told me these villains were afraid of neither man nor devil. They killed old Juan to get the secret. The paper they got was a hoax, and they'll soon found it out."

"But how could those ignorant brutes tell if it was a hoax when it was in cypher?"

"Are they ignorant, old chap? The Honorable may be a big blackguard, but in spite of his silly drawl, he's a gentleman and educated. He's Santley's grandson, and Santley was a gentleman. That oily Dutchman is no fool. They have brains among them as well as vice. Gaskara warned me especially against Hans Vanderlet. I respect those fellows. They'd knife us for the mere pleasure of it. Don't get them gaoled, for they'll hunt us down when they come out. Won't have it, Hector. I'm a bit fond of myself."

"Are you giving up then?"

"Giving up what? I was not aware I had started anything. Probably it would not be difficult to seize the gang, but would it be worthwhile? Such fearless desperadoes would never forget or forgive. They would swear a vendetta against us as they had sworn it against Black Juan Gaskara." He waved one hand and turned to leave. "They've got it, and I hope they are satisfied. If they obtain the treasure they'll go to ruin all the quicker."

"I know you, Jack. You don't mean that."

"I rather do."

"'Some day, if Heaven so wills, a good man will find this vast treasure and use it only for a good purpose. Such is my wish and prayer,'" Hector said.

Jack spun around. "What did you say?"

"That's what was written on that scrap of linen you took from Gaskara." Hector slowly walked to Jack. "'Some day, if Heaven so wills, a good man will find this vast treasure and use it only for a good purpose. Such is my wish and prayer.' You went to Gaskara's assistance when he was attacked by those ruffians but you did not have to. You returned to him, because you gave him your word, not because you had to. You wanted to help him, a stranger, albeit with the emphasis on 'strange,' but you did not have to. You're a good man, Jack. Just think, just imagine. To what good purposes could you employ that treasure? Agnes' hospital could put some of it to good use certainly. And what about Marsden, the waterman who helped you when you lived on the barge? There must be many, many more in this vast, sometimes pitiless city you could help. Do you toss all of them in the dustbin? Why? For what? For revenge? Just so those villains go to ruin quicker?"

"Damn your memory," Jack whispered. He was silent for a long time, the grandfather clock in the hall marking off the seconds. Hector's speech let Jack's memory retrieve another missing piece. Gaskara wanted him to have this secret. Giving Jack the treasure to use for good was Gaskara's last grasp at some kind of redemption, of trying to make amends in some small way for all the misery and death he had caused over his lifetime. Jack could do that. He wanted to do that. And maybe, just maybe, doing so would somehow help exorcise his uncle's ghost.

He wasn't looking at Hector; rather, he stared into a corner of the library as he thought. He finally met Hector's gaze. He pointed to the parchment. "We start tomorrow."

CHAPTER NINE

"**A**re you going to work on your old tub?" Marsden asked as he rowed Jack to the *Etruria*.

"I miss the old girl," Jack said. He patted the toolbox on his lap. "I'm going to spruce her up. Try to make her more seaworthy."

Jack paid Marsden when they reached the *Etruria,* then hopped on board. "Hector should be along directly."

"Right. I'll keep my eyes peeled." Marsden waved as he pushed off.

Jack returned the wave and looked around the deck, hands on hips. It was nice to be back onboard. He picked up his toolbox and went into the cabin, placing it on the table. He opened the box, and pulled the parchment out from between the tools.

After Vanderlet's visitation last night, Jack suggested working on the parchment away from his house and any more potential uninvited guests. Hector agreed, and the *Etruria* seemed like the perfect spot.

Jack lit the coal stove to take the chill out of the cabin. He filled a kettle with water and put it on the paraffin stove.

"Well, I'm supposed to working," Jack said, "so let's keep up appearances."

He went back on deck, and scrambled up the mast rigging. About an hour later, he heard a hail from Hector. He returned the greeting. Hector climbed on deck as Marsden pulled away.

"Come on up and enjoy the view!" Jack called.

"No, you come down. I'm not a creature of the air," Hector replied. "I worked in the bottom of the ship for a reason."

Jack laughed and nimbly made his way back to the deck.

"You are proof of Darwin's theory that we descended from apes," Hector observed. "You climbed down like a monkey."

Jack clapped Hector on his back. "You should have seen me when I had a tail!"

The two went into the cabin. Hector put the toolbox he was carrying on the table and opened it. Instead of tools, it contained pads of blank paper, pencils and a small English-Portuguese dictionary. Jack picked it up and inquired Hector with a look.

"I picked that up at in a bookstore on Charing Cross Road on the way over. Gaskara was Portuguese, was he not? It might be helpful. However, English or Portuguese, I still say there is no such thing as truly secret writing. Therefore, we should be able to solve this cryptogram."

Hector put the toolboxes on the deck and arranged the paper and pencils on the table. Jack moved to the stove and started the tea.

"However, a man may write a thing as a memorandum for himself which is an unsolvable puzzle to anyone else, if he merely writes it as a spur to his memory," Jack argued.

Hector thought for a moment. "I will concede that point."

"Hurrah!"

"Don't be cheeky," Hector replied. "An ordinary cryptogram can be read. The key is all we need. Gaskara gave you no key, and yet he wanted you to secure the treasure. The old pirate felt confident that you had ingenuity enough to discover the key."

"Keep moving, old chap," laughed Jack as he poured out the tea. "I see you're wound up."

"All secret writings are based on the same principle," went on Hector; "that is some sign or symbol replaces the original letters of the alphabet. They may be numbers, splashes, spots — anything, in fact. In this case old Juan chose pictures of objects familiar to him. Look at the parchment. It is a jumble of skulls, fish, guns, pistols, swords, daggers, ships, lighthouses, telescopes, anchors, and human faces. I should think it not very difficult. As I said before, an imperfectly educated sea-dog like Gaskara would hardly be the man to devise anything startling."

Jack brought a mug of tea to Hector. "Ah, but a cryptogram may be written backwards, upside down, in a star, circle, and so forth, and these methods add to the difficulty. And it may be written in any language."

"True, O king; but old Juan would use either English or Portuguese. The first step is to tabulate the different symbols and about how many times each occurs. Do you feel like taking a smack at it?"

"I'll pick it up, old boy, and I'll let you know." Jack picked up the parchment as Hector sat at the table. "Ready?"

Hector picked up a pencil and readied a pad of blank paper. He nodded.

[A series of cryptographic symbols spanning eight lines, followed by a boxed sequence of symbols]

Jack called out each symbol on the parchment while Hector tallied each one. Finally, Jack sat on the bunk while Hector finished counting up the symbols.

"I got the numbers out," Hector sighed as he sat back and stretched. "Neither of us knows any Portuguese, so let's start with the idea that Black Juan Gaskara wrote in plain English. If he did, I think we can knock spots out of this in no time. I have made my table roughly. It may not be quite accurate, but it can be put right later on. Ready?"

"Set all sail, my Hector," said Jack.

"Well, we'll begin. My calculation, as I warned you, may not be quite exact. The cryptogram contains 213 characters. We can divide them up as follows, beginning from the skull and reading forward in the ordinary way." Hector showed

Jack his chart of how many times each symbol occurred. "This gives us twenty-two separate symbols." Hector tapped his pencil on the table. "Our alphabet contains twenty-six letters. Presuming if Juan wrote in English, he would hardly use all the letters in a short message. X, z, v, and probably q would not be needed much."

"Whatever language he wrote, the cryptogram is very short," Jack observed.

"Your reasons for that statement, my wise youth?" asked Hector.

"At once," replied Jack. "The symbols cannot represent separate words. The '70' and '8' appear only once, so they may be a longitude and latitude on the face of it. The other symbols cannot be words, for how could the same word be repeated twenty-three times, as in the anchor's case, and similarly in the case of the cannon?"

"True, old chap, and a clincher," agreed Hector. "Therefore they must each represent some letter, and therefore the writing is short. Call the total number of letters 213, and allow the small average of, say, five letters to each word. Five divides into 218 forty-two times, with three over. So there cannot be more than fifty words in the cypher all told."

Jack nodded. He gestured to Hector, took the seat, picking up a pen and a clean sheet of paper.

"Now to weed it down," Hector went on as he examined his chart. "We'll start backwards. The moon, ship, and 132 occur least frequently, and letters seldom frequent in written and spoken English are v, p, y, s, and also b on odd occasions. The keg comes five times, the gallows seven. These may be m and f."

Jack wrote these on his paper.

Hector paced around the cabin as he continued. "The English letter occurring most frequently is e, another is t, and s and t are fond of coming together. Thousands of words begin st, such as in stag, sting, and end st or ts." He stared at the parchment. "The cannon appears twenty-two times, the anchor twenty-three. Which of these is e? Examine carefully. You will notice how frequently the anchor and the dancing man come together, and how rarely cannon and man meet. S and t are brothers, so to speak, and in my view we must call the cannon e, and the man and anchor st."

The two continued, suggesting, discussing, debating and arguing over what symbol could represent what letter. They finally reached the last one.

"A fish represents a or o." Jack noted their last agreement. He pointed at the parchment."Wait, what about the lighthouse? What has it done to be forgotten?"

"Hang it!" Hector exclaimed, "I thought we missed something. It is repeated eleven times. What haven't we got?"

"An l; we don't seem to have one," said Jack, glancing at his notes. He added the letter to his list. "Next move, please, old chap?"

"To make our alphabet," answered Hector. "So far we have done this, though we may be wrong. Let's write this down. Move."

Hector sat in the chair after Jack got out, and began creating a chart of the symbols and letters they represent.

"It probably contains many minor blunders," said Jack as he made two more mugs of tea. "Although a minor blunder could easily be rectified. The two great questions are these: Was our method the right one, and had the old corsair written in English?"

"We shall put our alphabet to the test to find out," said Hector, his face glowing with excitement. "That will give us the answer."

Hector diligently began to substitute letters for the parchment's symbols, mumbling to himself as he made the substitutions. His face fell in blank dismay when he finished. He handed Jack his work, like a student handing in a shoddy piece of school work.

Jack looked at the meaningless result, and began to laugh. "Is it in Choctaw, old chap?"

"Double Dutch or ancient Assyrian," commented Hector dryly as he took the page back. "We must have started — why, I say —"

Hector jumped up with triumphant yell and punched the air with his fist. "Cape!" he roared. "C-a-p-e, cape! The skull's c, not w, the moon p, not b. Hurrah, Jack, my old skeptic. The flag is b, and the fish a. Here goes again. Naturally the telescope is o."

"More power to you. You beat Hector of Troy. Cape makes sense, and it looks all right. Slip along."

Their excitement trebled. Jack caught the infection badly as he and Hector began to exchange letters for symbols. Hours passed. Copy after copy was flung aside, doubtful letters — q, z, x, j — were discarded and then tried time after time. Their enthusiasm was dashed over and over as promising combinations of letters failed a few symbols later. Wads of crumpled-up paper littered the floor. Singly or together, they took turns on deck to escape the closeness of the cabin. They sometimes compulsively cleaned the *Etruria* and once even engaged in an on-deck, bare-knuckle sparring match just to burn off their frustration before returning to their task. It was early evening when finally both men were eagerly bending over the result of their labor. The muddle of letters seemed to be forming, almost reluctantly, as though unwilling to give up their secret, into patterns which could be discerned as words.

The single group of letters at the bottom screamed one word: HEAT.

"It is in English!" Jack cried out. "The word lined round blackly at the bottom of the jumble of letters is enough to prove that."

They could not wait. The two huddled over the paper, grabbed pencils, and went to work again to arrange the jumble into words, shouting to each other excitedly as they teased another word from the pile of letters. It was simple enough in parts, but still Juan Gaskara's parchment was not clear.

Cape Bone 70 n 8 w e Clr May sight Flame Mt
Gtsku 13 2 lo 4. Bear east wth gt sku 13 2
lo 4 port wtch for blo2d wter hrk fo
B night seals thunder watch for floating
g driftweed mark drift steer whtie
g t es with led going steadily current strong smoke
2 right long ice
shore walrus dwel2
HEAT

Hector wiped the perspiration from his forehead and began to compare the translation with the parchment. "What on earth is the 13, 2 and the 4, Jack?"

Jack thought for a moment. "I think the 2's are plain enough, old chap. Look at 'dwel2.' It must mean repeat the previous letter. Then we get 'dwell.' 'Blo2d' is the same. Repeat the o and we have blood. And, by Jove, hero's the 4. Count from the skull on the chart — skull, fish, moon, cannon. The cannon is e. 'Ic4' means ice. Good biz, again! The lighthouse is the thirteenth hieroglyph, and the lighthouse stands for l. Thirteen twice must be doubled. Try it. He's missed a few vowels out, too, I see. He's also left out some words, like a telegram."

The mystery stood revealed as Hector filled out Gaskara's abbreviations and added words to make sentences:

Cape Bone, 70 n 8 w Clear (in) May. sight Flame
Mountain (and) great skull ice. Bear East with great
skull ice (to) port. Watch for blood-water (and) hark
for night-seals' thunder. Watch for floating driftweed;
mark drift (and) steer (through or for?) white
gates with (the) lead going steadily. (The) current
(is) strong (and) smokes. Sight (the) long iceshore
(where the) walrus dwell.
HEAT.

Hector handed the translation to Jack. The quaint wording of it spoke of strange lands and a past age. The blood-water, the current that smoked, the thunder of the seals, and the white gates — what did the N mean? Where or what was Cape Bone? What was the great skull ice, and the long ice shore where the walruses dwelt?

"It's a frost," said Jack gloomily. "It tells us nothing at all. There's nothing to go upon. It's too utterly vague."

"Where is Cape Bone? I've never heard of it," said Hector.

"It may be something Gaskara named himself, or that it's a name not used anymore," suggested Jack.

"Not a bad shot. How about the 70 n and 8 w?"

"70 n 8 w," Jack pondered. "That could be latitude and longitude: 70 north 8 west."

"Where on earth is that?"

Jack shrugged. "There's an atlas at home in the library. We could look it up."

"What does he mean by 'heat'?" asked Hector. "The island is hot?"

"Heat ... heat," Jack thought for a moment, then brightened. He waved the parchment in the air. "Heat! Heat!"

Jack charged over to the stove. He grabbed the handle of the tea kettle. He yelped, let go of the hot handle and grabbed a towel. He wrapped the towel around the handle and slid the kettle off. He held the parchment over the hot stove.

"Heat! It's not a description, it is an instruction!" he cried. "Hector!"

Hector sprang to his side. Something began to creep out on the old surface. Th e fi gures and drawing fl ashed out stronger and more distinct:

⼟✕⟁ᴵⁱᵉ ⁷ᵉ𝟢𝟢 ⼋𝟢ₗₛ✕ 𝘤⟁𝟢𝟢𝕀 𝟢⼟𝕀 ᴓₗₛ✕. ⁷⼋𝟢 ⼟𝟢⟁ᴓ⼟⼋⼋𝟢⟁ ᴓₗₛᴓ✕⼋𝟢 ⼋ₗₛ ⼤✕𝟢ᴓ𝘤ₗₛ⟁𝕀𝕀 ⌐ᴓ𝟢⟁.

⌐⟁⼋ᴓ𝟢𝟢 ⼤✕ᴓᴓ≏, ✕𝟢⼤ ⼊ᴓ⼟⟁ ᴓₗₛ✕ ᴓᴓ⼋𝕀✕𝟢⼋ₗₛ. ⼟⼋ 𝕀𝕀⟁⁷⼤, ⁷𝕀ᴓᴓ𝘤⼋𝕀⟁ ⼋ₗₛ ✕⼋⼋⁷⟁,

𝘤⼋𝕀𝕀 ✕⼋⼋ₗₛ ⼤⼊⼋ₗₛ⟁⼤ ⼋𝟢⼟✕ ᴓᴓ𝟢⟁. ✕⟁✕✕𝟢 𝘤⼋𝟢ₗₛ⼤⼤ ⼤⼟𝟢ᴓ𝟢⼤✕⼟ ᴓ⼟ ⁷⼋𝟢 ✕⼋ₗₛ✕𝟢⟁✕

𝘤ᴓ𝟢⟁⼤. ✕𝟢⼋⼤⟁ ✕⟁𝟢⟁, ⼊⼋⼊ ⼤✕ᴓ𝕀𝕀 ⁷𝟢ₗₛ✕ ⼋ₗₛ𝕀⟁⼤⼤ ⼟✕⟁ ᴓᴓₗₛ ᴓ𝘤⟁⼤ ✕ᴓ∨⟁

✕⟁⼤⼟𝟢⼋ᴓ⟁✕, 𝟢⁷⼤⼋⼋⟁ ⼊⼋⼋𝟢 𝕀ᴓ⌐⼋𝟢 𝟢⼤ ∨ᴓ⼊ₗₛ⟁.—▲⼊.

"It's true," gasped Hector.

"Gaskara made use of some chemical ink whose image would be developed by ink," yelled Jack, "like a photographic plate being developed!"

The next moment both men, their pulses throbbing, were staring at another wild medley of hieroglyphs, and at a map of the land of mystery — Peril Island.

CHAPTER TEN

As they watched, the map and lower medley of hieroglyphs began to fade from the parchment.

"It only wants heating again, I hope," said Jack.

He went back to the stove. He was right. The mysterious pictures slowly crept out, increasing in density and blackness, until they were perfectly strong and clear. It was a simple matter to complete the translation.

"Put the lot together," said Jack, "and read it aloud."

Hector read slowly, filling in missing words and stumbling over some of the archaic spellings: "Cape Bone 70 north, 8 east. Clear (of ice) In May. Sight the Flame Mountain and the Great Skull Ice. Bear east with the Great Skull Ice to port. Watch for the blood water and hark for the night thunder. Watch for floating drift weed and mark the drift. Steer through the White Gates with the lead going steadily. The current is strong and smookes. Sight the long ice-shore where the sea elephants dwell. (Heat.) Then fair wind Peril Island. For treasure anchor on Shrapnell Baye, Bewair Shark, his Gate and Cauldron. To left, flagpole on Hoofe, Pull down stones with care. Hedde points straight at four hundred paces. Digge here, you shall find unless the weather have destroyed, If'soe your labor is vayne.–J.G."

The map, roughly but cleverly drawn, bore out the ghastly story of Seth Lake. Black Juan had marked the scenes of many horrid tragedies, as if he had reveled in his crimes.

"Here I shotte Eph. Vanderlet."
"Here Lake was killed."
"Here I sank the boats."
"Here I shotte J. Guerin."
"Here I found Santley's body."

Each line was a whole tale of human agony and horror. They stared fascinated at the chart of the island of mystery drawn by Black Juan's blood-stained hand.

They remained silent, examining the map, Jack peering over Hector's shoulder. Hector read it over several more times. He put it down, and looked at Jack.

They burst into hoots of laughter, pounding each other on the back and dancing around the cabin.

"It's like a book! It's like a book!" Jack cried out. "We found a treasure map!"

"We have to get it first!" Hector called back.

"Minor detail! Minor detail!" Jack yelled.

They continued to celebrate until they were exhausted. Jack flopped onto the bunk and Hector collapsed on the chair.

They finally caught their breath. After a quiet moment, Hector spoke.

"I'm hungry," he complained.

Jack realized they hadn't eaten since breakfast. "Me, too. I feel a little nervous carrying this map around town. You go back to the house, raid the kitchen for something to eat and bring it back here. Be sure to put things away, or Mrs. Clare will have a fit. We'll stay on the *Etruria* tonight, since nobody knows we're here. Then we'll take the parchment to the bank vault tomorrow morning."

Hector leaped up. "Right. I'll be back in two shakes."

Hector left the cabin. Jack heard him whistle for a boatman. Jack stared at the translation in his hand.

Jack sat at the table and found a clean sheet of paper, and copied the translation in his best schoolboy's hand. Satisfied with his work, he checked around the cabin for a hiding place. He rolled up the threadbare rug. He picked up the lamp and knelt on the deck. He pried up a loose floorboard.

The lamplight reflected in the greasy bilgewater below. Jack felt along the next joist over, and found a section where the floorboard warped up slightly, leaving a small gap. He folded his copy of the parchment in fourths, then slipped it in the space between the floorboard and the joist. He replaced the floorboard and rolled the rug back over it.

"Safer than the Bank of England," Jack grinned as he patted the floor.

Jack got up and cleaned up the wads of paper that lay scattered about. He had finished when he started to wonder what was keeping Hector. There was a slight bump and grating sound as a boat came alongside the *Etruria*.

"It's about time!" Jack called out. He heard some shuffling outside the door, then silence. He went to the door and pulled it open. "Well, what are you waiting for? An engraved invitation?"

Hector stood in the doorway, semi-conscious, swaying slightly. He was gagged, and bound hand and foot. His shirt had been ripped open and pulled back over his shoulders. A cross in the center of two concentric circles was painted on his chest.

"Hector!" Jack exclaimed. He caught Hector as he toppled forward and lowered him to the floor.

Standing in the doorway behind Hector was Monkey Swayne, mouthing, leering, and chuckling. Behind him loomed the fat figure of Vanderlet, an evil grin on his face and a leveled revolver in each puffy hand. For what seemed an eternity of time there was neither sound nor movement.

"What have you done to him?" Jack angrily demanded.

"He is not hurt badly," Vanderlet said with no concern.

"Burn me," hissed Monkey Swayne, "we're good enough for him, Hans."

"That is so," Vanderlet cooed softly. "Be not afraid, be not afraid. I am a man of peace, and I hate trouble. Mr. Drayton, not a word, not a sound. But," Vanderlet added with a hideous smile, "if you do not do what I say, I will plaster the wall with your brains. Hands over your head. Slowly. We come in."

Jack raised his hands. "I suppose you do."

He stepped backward as Vanderlet and Swayne came into the cabin.

"We call at your house this evening," Vanderlet said. "We do not find you or find the paper. Then luck, your friend stops by, and he tells of the wonderful work you do today, and where you are."

"Dancin' a few rounds with a red-hot poker loosed his tongue," Swayne cackled.

Vanderlet smiled indulgently. "Yes. Your friend finally did not want to lose his eyes."

"How long is this going to last? Tonight?" asked Jack.

"Ach," said Vanderlet, "that is the question we have to arrange. Mine friend, I love a man that can smile in adversity. To the point: the paper was a cursed forgery. I do not like looking the fool."

"That was not our fault. You are the ones who took it," reminded Jack. "You did a good job making yourself look like the fool without any help from me."

A look of savage anger flickered across Vanderlet's usually bland face. "Monkey, you will take the paper and walk backwards to me."

"We'll win tonight or swing!" crowed Swayne. He grabbed the parchment and translation off the table, and stuffed them in his pocket. He backed to Vanderlet.

"Tell me one thing, Vanderlet. Are you doing all of this for the treasure's monetary value? After all, you're rich enough. Or is it to revenge your ancestor after all these years?" Jack asked.

"It is not for either," replied Vanderlet. "It is for opportunity."

"Opportunity? Opportunity for what?"

Vanderlet smiled. "Piracy of Gaskara's day is dead but piracy still is alive. Robbery, blackmail, embezzlement, narcotics, murder. By using Gaskara's treasure, I bring all today's pirates of the world under one command — my command. I protect them from the local authorities. I find targets. For this service, they pay me a tiny part of their income."

"As tribute?" asked Jack sarcastically.

"As a *fee*, you understand. I dispose of those who do not agree to my leadership or are not of use. With the treasure, that power is now within my grasp."

"That all sounds very ambitious, but you will pardon me if I don't wish you luck."

"Which brings us to this present situation," Vanderlet cooed. "It is difficult, but you will understand. Now, mine friend, be sensible, pray be sensible. We have all to lose but little to win. Therefore, we are desperate men. You may shout and bring help, but the trouble it will bring! We shoot you all, I swear. We shoot and shoot and shoot. But we are no common thieves. No, no, no. We take only one little scrap of paper. We have what we want, and we wish to go. Will you let us go? Will you give your word as a gentleman that we have twenty minutes before you give the alarm?"

"No, you oily thief," Jack replied.

"Sink me," snarled Swayne, "put a bullet through each of the dogs and run for it."

"Mine heart too tender," said Vanderlet. He smiled. "I could not."

"Then I will." Swayne leveled his weapons.

"You may just wish to reconsider," Jack said.

"And why is that?" Vanderlet asked politely.

"I posted a letter to my solicitor this morning," Jack said, "explaining everything that has happened to me, up to and including last night's incident. It is complete with names, dates and descriptions. If my body is found with a bullet in it, I am sure my solicitor will become most suspicious, and turn that letter over to the police."

Vanderlet smiled sadly and shook his head. "A very old trick, Mr. Drayton."

Jack returned the smile. "A very old trick, Mr. Vanderlet, but nevertheless a very good old trick, since there is no way for you to check its veracity."

"Oh, but there is a way," said Vanderlet. He motioned with his gun. "Be so kind to remove your shirt and sit in that chair."

"I keep in mind all the time that a man without a gun can't fight a man with a gun," Jack said as he complied with Vanderlet's orders. He was gratified that the same calm voice he mustered while in Gaskara's room had returned. "So be polite, tell him what a fine fellow he is, and promise to do everything he wants."

"You speak wise," Vanderlet said. "Monkey, take that rope in the corner. Get Mr. Drayton ready to answer questions."

Jack sat in the chair. He couldn't suppress a shudder in anticipation of what was likely to come. He resolved to make it as hard as possible for Vanderlet to get any information, but at the same time he didn't know how long he could last. Oddly, he also had a detached curiosity about how much he could take, and if could he take as much as Hector, as though casually being interested in the results of a sporting match. He steeled himself.

Swayne pulled Jack's hands to the back and tied them, then pulled two loops of rope around Jack's midsection. He winced as Swayne tightened them so much as to bite into his skin, then tied them to the chair back. Swayne moved in front of Jack, grinning, and pulled out his knife. He eyed Jack as if he were a prize goose, ready to be carved for the holiday meal. He pricked the point of his knife in Jack's side, and slowly twisted it back and forth. Jack sucked in his breath. Swayne pulled the knife out. A drop of blood bubbled to the surface and trickled down Jack's skin.

"The police most likely will not regard your involvement, Vanderlet, no matter what the letter says. Inspector Tasker has already made that clear," began Jack.

Swayne placed the knife blade on Jack's breastbone. He pressed down and began to cut slowly. Jack uttered a sharp cry of pain and grimaced. "So Vanderlet will not be bothered by the police," Jack gasped out. "But what about you, Swayne? And Guerin, and Lake? Do you truly think Vanderlet will protect you? Why should he? Why would he?"

Swayne stopped cutting and stepped back. Jack felt his warm blood dripping down his torso. He caught his breath and continued. "Do you think he will lie to the police to save you? No, he'd turn you over to the police to save his own skin. You can be replaced. All of you can be. You heard him. He will dispose of those he doesn't need."

Swayne nervously shifted his weight, his hand tightening and loosening on the knife. He licked his lips. "Burn you," he said without much conviction. He raised his knife again.

"Think about it," Jack continued urgently and rapidly, to stop Vanderlet from interrupting. "What if my body and Hector's body are discovered, both bearing the marks of torture? Or what if we simply disappeared? In either case, there certainly would be questions raised. Even if there wasn't a letter, although there is, my solicitor would most certainly contact the police. Even the plodding Inspector Tasker may take interest, and recall what I told him in the hospital. Would Vanderlet want to be involved with anything like that? A man of his social status and wealth? No, of course not, so he will point to you and the others to deflect attention from himself. Who do you think the police would believe? You or him? I can tell you the answer, because I've had experience with that. Inspector Tasker did not believe me, and he certainly will not believe you. For you Swayne, it would be a long walk to the gallows, a climb up thirteen steps, followed by a short, sharp drop."

Swayne whirled around to face Vanderlet.

Vanderlet stared at Jack with a trace of admiration. "You are the most cool customer I ever meet," he said quietly. "Perhaps you are right. Marks of violence interest the police. But a sad accident only bring sympathy."

Vanderlet nodded toward the stove. Swayne laughed and put away his knife. Wrapping Jack's shirt around his hands, he charged the stove.

"I'm goin' to burn you, roast you alive," croaked Swayne. "That's what I'm goin' to do."

Swayne aimed a shove at the coal stove. It crashed over, the pipes came down with a clanging rattle, and a mass of hissing coals rolled over the floor amid a cloud of smoke. Laughing, Swayne unwrapped his hands and tossed Jack's shirt on the coals. It smoldered, smoked, and burst into flames. Then he grabbed the paraffin stove, and dashed it to the floor also, adding more fuel to the fire.

"I am glad, I am glad," Vanderlet murmured, "I am glad I not shoot you. Keep the police away. Good night, good night."

Swayne picked up the lamp and threw it at the burning shirt. With a whooshing roar, a fireball shot toward the ceiling. Vanderlet and Swayne sprang out the cabin door, slamming it shut.

Jack tore at his bonds to no effect. He rocked back and forth, finally awkwardly gaining his feet, the chair still tied to him like a turtle's shell. He ran backwards, smashing the chair into a wall. He heard snapping sounds as he tumbled back to the floor. Grunting, he managed to get to his feet and find his balance again. He went backwards into the wall once more with all the force he could muster. The chair splintered into pieces as Jack slid down the wall to the floor.

The cabin filled with choking, blinding smoke. Jack threw off the remains of the chair and walked on his knees to his toolbox. He sat with his back to it, and fumbled to open it. He grabbed and tossed out tool after tool, until he found what he wanted: a small coping saw.

Jack glanced toward Hector. He was fully conscious now, and struggling against the ropes. Jack scooted over to him.

"Hector, roll over with your back to me. I'm going to give you this saw. Hang onto it as tightly as you can."

Hector rolled over, and Jack placed the saw's handle in Hector's hands, serrated edge pointing up.

"Grasp it tightly, as tightly as you can," Jack urged.

Jack rubbed the rope tying his hands back and forth across the saw teeth. He paused as a smoke-induced coughing fit seized him for a short while, then returned to cutting the rope. He felt it loosen, and he jerked his hands free.

He pulled the saw out of Hector's hands and untied them. Blinking away the tears from his smarting eyes, he then freed Hector's feet.

Jack looked at where he hid his copy of the parchment. The rug was burning like tinder, and the less inflammable floorboards were slowly blistering.

"Get some water! Use the bucket on deck!" he ordered Hector.

Jack grabbed a piece of the chair leg, and dropped down to the floor to stay below the smoke as much as possible. He crawled toward the loose floorboard.

The heat drove him back. Gritting his teeth, he moved forward again on his belly. It was as if he was crawling into a furnace.

He reached the rug. Using the chair leg, he flipped the burning rug away from the floorboard. The fire's intense heat seemed to be searing the skin off his bones, and he screamed at the pain.

Water splashed over him, bringing him some relief. The smoke thinned slightly and some flames extinguished with an angry hiss.

"More! More!" Jack yelled.

"Jack!"

"Get more water!" Jack shouted. He pried up the hot floorboard, burning his fingertips. He began to reach for his copy of the parchment.

Suddenly Jack was being pulled back by his feet. He clawed at that floor in a vain attempt to stop himself.

"No! No! I almost had it!" he yelled. "Let me loose! Let me go!"

Hector pulled Jack off the floor, pinning his arms behind him. Jack fought like a madman as Hector hustled him to the door.

"No! You don't understand! I have to get it!" he raged.

Hector pulled Jack out of the cabin and almost threw him to the deck. Jack ended up on all fours. The fire had eaten through some of the roof beams. With a crackling roar, the roof collapsed, burying where Jack had been in a pile of flaming debris.

"I almost had it. I almost had it!" Jack pounded the deck with his fists in anger and frustration.

"What? What did you almost have?"

"A copy I made of the parchment. I could have had it if you hadn't pulled me away," Jack spat out angrily.

"Jack, the roof was about to fall in. You would have been killed," Hector said.

Jack sighed and placed his forehead against the deck. "Yes, yes. I know. You're right. I'm sorry."

"Jack! Hector!" A voice called from off the port side.

"It's Marsden," Hector said, helping Jack to his feet. "We have to abandon ship."

Jack and Hector dove off the *Etruria* and swam the few strokes to Marsden's boat. They pulled themselves in.

"Are you two all right?" asked Marsden.

Jack nodded.

"The fireboat is almost here," Marsden said, pointing to the steam-powered launch nearing the burning *Etruria*. "They should be able to save her. What happened?"

"An accident with the stove," Jack answered. He started to shiver, not only because of the night's cold.

"Let me take you to my house to dry off," Marsden said as he put his oars in the water.

Jack smiled gratefully. "Thank you, Marsden. You're a brick."

Marsden took Jack and Hector to his little cottage. He gave them blankets to wrap themselves in as he hung their clothes to dry by the fire. He finally deposited Jack and Hector on the small settee before he donned his pea-coat.

"I'll go back and see about the *Etruria*. Now don't stir out till I get back," the good-natured waterman said with mock sternness. "If you don't promise, I'll not go."

Jack chuckled. "Then we promise. This is splendid of you, Marsden. I'll raise your pay."

Marsden laughed and left. Jack and Hector sat in silence for a long time, staring into the fireplace. Hector finally spoke.

"I'm sorry, Jack," he said quietly.

"About what?"

"I brought Vanderlet and Swayne to the *Etruria*. I didn't want to, but when they threatened to blind me, putting that glowing poker an inch from my eye, I couldn't ..." His voice trailed off. He shook his head in dismay. "They were *laughing* about it."

"Hector, please, you have no need to apologize," Jack said. "You had no choice. I'm sorry you were … you went through what you did." Jack noted the burn marks on Hector's chest and stomach. "Is it still painful?"

Hector nodded.

"They've got my back up, Hector. But, oh, wouldn't I like to do them out of the treasure." Jack got up and paced the floor. "They've got the chart, and the copy is most likely destroyed, so it's all up."

"Would you go if you had the parchment?"

"Yes, of course, but —"

Hector stood. "You *would* go."

"You seem pretty keen, Hector."

"Keen?" Hector walked up to Jack. "I'm mustard itself. Well, would you go if you had the parchment?"

"Yes, yes. I just said I would. I would love to upend Vanderlet's little plan of grandeur," Jack was quiet for a second. Then he spoke firmly. "And, more importantly, carry out Gaskara's wishes. I want to employ that ill-gotten gain for some good, maybe leave this world in a little better shape than when I found it. But without —"

Hector closed his eyes and started reciting. "Cape Bone 78 north, 8 east. Clear of ice in May. Sight the Flame Mountain and the Great Skull Ice. Bear east with the Great Skull Ice to port. Watch for the blood water and hark for the night thunder. Watch for floating drift weed and mark the drift. Steer through the White Gates with the lead going steadily.'" He opened his eyes. "Need I go on?"

"Damn your memory!" Jack cried as he grabbed Hector by his shoulders.

"Get me some paper and a pencil so I can write it down," Hector said, holding out his hands. "The language is so unusual, not to mention the pain I'm in, that I may lose part of it."

Jack rummaged around in a small table until he found a small notebook and the stub of a pencil. He handed them to Hector.

Hector took the items and sat. He scribbled down the words automatically, almost as if they were being dictated, repeating them to himself. When he finished, he handed the paper to Jack.

"I can remember every word, but I can't draw that map from memory without a slip, though," Hector added apologetically.

"No need to worry!" Jack said, reading over the paper.

"First, we need to charter a boat," Hector said.

"No, I don't think so."

"What do you mean?"

"Bringing more people into this business may munge things up," Jack said. "The more who know about the treasure, the more possibility of trouble."

"True." Hector nodded then he snapped his fingers. "The *Enigma!*"

"What? What's an enigma?"

"Remember I told you I worked on a fishing boat?"

"Yes. You said the captain took sick."

"That's correct. I think I can get use of the boat ... the *Enigma.*"

"How —" Jack started.

Hector cut him off. "I'll leave for Cornwall on the first train in the morning. I'm sure my old captain and I can come to a mutually acceptable agreement."

"If you say so. Leave me a list of things for me to procure at this end. It's April 14. Gaskara wrote that the area around Peril Island isn't clear of ice until May. That gives us at least two weeks to prepare."

"Be ready to come immediately after I wire you," Hector said.

"Of course," Jack said. He paused for a second then cried out: "Success to Peril Island!"

Hector left early the next morning, leaving a multi-page list on the library table. Later that day, Jack and Marsden went to check on the *Etruria*. They found her moored to a stake, lying behind a large Brazilian steamer. They jumped on board. Jack sadly gazed at the barge's condition. The cabin was completely gutted. The floor was simply not there anymore. Any shred of hope that his copy of the map survived left Jack.

"She's still afloat at least, Jack," said Marsden positively. "It looks like mostly the cabin was damaged. The fireboat did a good job."

"Yes," Jack agreed. The barge seemed doleful and abandoned. "The *Etruria* was the first thing I ever owned, other than the clothes on my back. She deserves better."

He thought for a moment, then pulled out his billfold. He handed Marsden a handful of bills. "Dock your boat, Marsden. I'm now officially hiring you to supervise the *Etruria's* repair. I want her fixed up as good as the day she was launched. Do you think you can manage it?"

Marsden grinned. "Of course I can!

Jack slapped Marsden on his back and laughed. "I knew you could! I may be gone for a time. I don't know for how long, so I'll arrange a draft at the bank so you can draw the funds you need. When I get back, I expect the *Etruria* to be ship-shape and Bristol fashion!"

"She will be, Jack, she will be!"

A week later, Jack and Agnes strolled arm-in-arm down the wide path in Hyde Park, through the dappled sunlight that shone through the huge trees.

"It's been a dreamy week," whispered Agnes.

Jack murmured in agreement. "You start medical school soon. You have a lot of work in front of you." He slipped his arm around her waist and pulled her closer. "I am so proud of you."

"It's a shame you have to go. I could use your help studying." Agnes giggled as she toyed with one of his shirt buttons. "Especially with the anatomy part."

Jack took her hand and kissed it. "You saw the wire. I received it this morning."

"I know Hector is a friend, but the telegram was so peculiar! Just a jumble of words ..."

"Head cannon fish X ship," Jack said. He laughed. "It is code: R E A D Y. Hector was being overly dramatic. I leave on the first train tomorrow."

"You don't know when you'll return?"

"No, I'm afraid not."

"But you will return?" Agnes gazed up at him.

Jack kissed her on her nose. "Of course I'll come back. It may take a month or so, but I'll come back. And maybe with a big surprise."

"Why? Why do you have to go?"

"I'm sorry, my love, but I can't tell you anymore."

"A secret mission," Agnes said with a nod of her head. She laid her head on his shoulder. "You're going on a secret mission."

"You will wait for me?"

"You don't need to ask," Agnes said. "Unless a handsome young medical student just happens to come along at college."

"Fickle, fickle, fickle," Jack grinned and shook his head.

They stopped, and Jack turned Agnes to face him. He leaned toward her.

Agnes nodded to the others walking down the path. "In front of an audience?"

Jack smiled. "Of course."

They kissed.

CHAPTER ELEVEN

Jack put his suitcase on the dock, and stared at the small boat in disbelief. Masts stood at either end, with a large tiller at the stern. A low cabin roof jutting about two feet above the deck and lined by small portholes took up the middle third of the deck. Hector emerged from the cabin hatchway and spotted Jack. He waved.

"Ahoy on the dock!" Hector spread his arms wide. "Behold the *Enigma*. What do you think of her?"

"How big is she?"

"Thirty-seven feet from bow to stern."

"This is going to get us to the island?" Jack asked doubtfully.

"The trouble with you is you are only used to large ocean liners. I'll have you know that in 1854, a lugger similar to this one sailed from Penzance all the way to Australia, a mere 12000 miles. And luggers like this are fast. Smugglers once used them to regularly outpace any Revenue vessel in service." Hector folded his arms. "You don't look convinced."

"I'm not entirely."

"Doubting Thomas! Come aboard, and I'll show you the ropes."

"I'm waiting for —" Jack turned around and pointed to two workmen pushing a dolly loaded with a wooden crate, " — them."

The puffing workmen pushed the dolly up Jack. He gestured to Hector. "Lend us a hand getting this on board."

The four heaved the crate onto the *Enigma's* deck. One workman leaned on the crate and fanned himself with his cap.

"Blimey!" he gasped, "what have you got in this bloody box?"

Jack pulled out his billfold and smiled. "A carronade."

Both workmen give Jack the same look, halfway between curious and suspicious. The looks disappeared after Jack's generous tips.

"Thank you kindly, sir." The workman tugged on his cap visor. "Pleasant day to you, sir."

The two workmen left, tossing a glance over their shoulders as they pushed their dolly away.

"So what is in the crate?" Hector leaned against it.

"A carronade."

"What!" Hector stood up straight.

"A 12-pounder actually. Consider it a christening gift for the *Enigma*."

"Why on earth did you bring —"

"Are we not searching for treasure?" Jack interrupted with a smile. "We need protection, do we not?"

"Well, it's here now," Hector sighed in resignation. "Where did you find it?"

"While I waited for your wire, I revisited Gaskara's room, hoping to uncover some additional clues," Jack said. "There I meet one very unhappy, barely sober, landlord, bitterly complaining that all of Gaskara's belongings remained unclaimed in the room. So I bought them all, lock, stock and barrel. That included this carronade, which I told the landlord was for a garden decoration, although I don't think he believed me."

Jack shrugged. "He was too busy counting the wonga I had put in his hand anyway. Old Juan had told me that there were 1000 guineas inside a stuffed shark, a rather unique safe, I must say. There was, so I used those funds to procure from, shall we say, perhaps legal sources some roundshot, a powder, ramrod, two rifles plus ammunition. All of which is packed in here. Oh, and I hung the stuffed shark in your bedroom."

"Very thoughtful of you."

"Don't mention it."

"Do you know how to fire one of those things?" Hector asked doubtfully as he pointed to the carronade.

Jack hedged. "I read up on how to."

"But you never actually did fire one," Hector pressed.

"I read quite a bit. Now who is not looking convinced?" Jack headed toward his suitcase. "In here, I also packed the Bible, works by Shakespeare, Wilde, and Plato. I assume the items I shipped ahead have already made it onboard."

He picked up his suitcase and returned to the grinning Hector. "I can't tell if you are more excited by the carronade or the books."

"Both, dear chap, both."

Over the next three days, Jack and Hector took the *Enigma* out as Hector taught Jack basic seamanship. They also fixed the carronade on deck forward of the cabin, hiding the weapon under the crate at Jack's suggestion to prevent any questions as to why a ship like the *Enigma* needed to carry armament.

On the second day, Jack scanned the horizon. No land or other craft was in sight. He pulled out the ramrod, a powder charge and shot. Then he pulled up a bucket of water from over the side.

Hector was manning the tiller, and watched the activity with great interest. "What are you doing?"

"I'm going to load this thing," Jack answered, "to prove to you that I can."

"You're not going to blow up the boat, will you?"

"That's always a possibly," Jack replied.

"How reassuring."

"First step, sponge out the barrel."

Jack soaked the sponge on the end the ramrod, and was about to push it down the barrel when he noticed something. He put down the sponge, reached in and pulled a piece of paper. It was covered in hieroglyphs. "Look," Jack said as he went over to Hector, "here is some more of Gaskara's artwork."

"Where did that come from?"

"It was stuffed inside the carronade." Jack thought for a minute. "Wait a minute. I think … I seem to recall Gaskara wrote this, then his parrot hid it in the carronade. Do you remember the alphabet?"

"I have it written in my notebook. It's down in the cabin." Hector took the cryptogram. "You take the helm and keep us on the same heading. I'll go below and translate this."

Jack took over the tiller, and Hector disappeared into the cabin. After about ten minutes, he reemerged, holding the paper in one hand and scratching his head with the other.

"Well, what does it say?" asked Jack.

"Translated, it says quote: 'Harsh mistress.' Unquote."

"Which means what?"

Hector shrugged. "I haven't the foggiest idea. Perhaps it is a warning, or a memory, or a comment on gold lust, or a raving from his unbalanced mind."

"Perhaps Peril Island is inhabited by a race of Amazon warrior women," suggested Jack.

"Well there's an interesting thought," Hector said, taking over the tiller. "Go back to your plaything."

Jack returned to the carronade, practicing the loading movements repeatedly, even with his eyes closed, much to Hector's great amusement. He ended up leaving the carronade loaded.

"I won't fire it off," Jack said.

"Be thankful for small mercies," replied Hector. "It is time to return to port. Put your toy away and prepare to show me how well you handle the sails."

Jack replaced the crate over the carronade and headed for the forward sail. Jack proved a ready learner, so by the time they reached the port Hector decided that they were ready to set sail after taking on final provisions.

The night before they planned to leave, Jack sat on the crate, staring off to the horizon. Hector came up to him.

"Hector," Jack said, with a note of concern in his voice, "this is where we ought to pause and think."

"Don't tire yourself, sonny," laughed Hector.

"Don't worry, I won't. We have a several hundred-mile voyage. Ahead of us lies the unknown, and I confess that the unknown can be fearful."

"You weren't fearful of the unknown when you walked out on your uncle."

Jack chuckled. "True. I was too angry at the time to consider anything but leaving. But now ... what shall we find? What good will it bring us? How long are we going to stay there? How are we going to get back?"

"One at a time, me lad, one at a time, for the love of pity," Hector answered. He paused, and became as serious as Jack had ever seen him. "Justice is justice. A man owns his own life if he owns nothing else. I'll go on as long as you like, but the moment either of us protests, we must agree to put our nose south again."

Jack thought for a second, then nodded.

"That settles it," Hector answered and put out his hand. "At the first protest, from either of us, we turn back."

They shook hands.

The *Enigma* left the harbor and headed north the next morning. Jack and Hector divided up chores and watches, and the small boat lived up to its reputation for speed. The days were almost hot, so warm that the two trod the deck barefoot and clad only in their trousers, reminding Jack how much he enjoyed being out on the ocean. It seemed like a pleasure cruise, and almost made him forget the purpose of their trip.

Over and over again they discussed Juan Gaskara's directions. The latitude and longitude of the old pirate seemed utterly impossible. What lay at the intersection of these two imaginary lines?

There was the passage "clear in May." Clear of what? The answer could only be ice. The "Flame Mountain" might some undiscovered volcano in the region. "The night seals' thunder" was definite enough, but what of the blood water, and the current that smoked? Their one hope was to push north and trust to time and luck to solve the mystery. Black Juan's directions were too hazy, vague, and indefinite to steer anything except a blind man's course by.

As the *Enigma* plowed north, the weather cooled. Jack and Hector bundled up in more and more clothes. One night, they stood on deck.

"By Jove," said Jack, pointing to the sky, "isn't that splendid?"

A fan of silver light flashed upwards in the northern sky. It filled the gray heavens, flushed from silver to yellow, to pink, to crimson, to dazzling gold, and then died out. Above them blazed the stars, and the chill breath of the eternal ice was wafted into their faces across the mysterious silence of the darkening sea.

The next day, they spotted their first iceberg far off their port bow. They stood on deck, watching in awe the monstrous mountain of gleaming ice floating along with towering majesty.

"Can you imagine what would happen if a ship collided with one of those? Even as large as the ones we crewed on?" asked Jack.

Hector shook his head. "I don't want to. How is it that we haven't seen more bergs? I thought these seas swarmed with them."

"Maybe a lack of icebergs means a cold summer," Jack suggested. "And here's another point. I think occasionally, but I don't talk a lot."

Hector cleared his throat.

"Quiet, callow youth." Jack continued, "How long was Juan on Peril Island? Years, he said. I can't remember all he told me, for I was in a funk. He ought to have had a tremendously long and dark winter, weeks and weeks of sunless days. He surely would have spoken of it. The disappearance of the sun would have left a strong impression on him. But he did not speak a single word on the point. How is Peril Island lighted in the dead months?"

"Odd. Juan had been used to a tropical sun. He must have commented on the terror of the arctic winter," muttered Hector. He shrugged. "I give it up. It's a riddle."

"Yet another one," added Jack.

Due to the possibility of icebergs, the two rearranged their watches so that one of them was on deck at all times. It was two days later Jack had a late watch. It was a moonless night, made even darker by an overcast which blotted out most of the stars. Held by her sea anchor, the *Enigma* seemed to ride the ocean in a vast black void, the only thing existing in the entire world.

Jack strode the deck in his old pea-coat, its warm familiarity a comfort. He blew on his hands to warm them, and stuck them in his coat pockets. He wondered if standing watch would make any difference tonight; it was so dark, he probably could only spot an iceberg if it were three feet off the bow. Despite the chill, he drank in the cold, keen air as he took another turn on the deck.

He stopped. He thought he heard something over the slap of the water on the *Enigma's* hull. He strained to listen, and he picked up the sound again: a low, dull throb, that seemed to be growing louder. Jack went down to the cabin and woke Hector.

"Iceberg?" asked Hector as he climbed out of his bunk.

Jack shook his head. "I don't know."

He started up the companionway, hesitated, then grabbed a loaded rifle and gave the second one to Hector.

"What are these for?" Hector said as he put on his jacket.

"I don't know."

"What do you know?" Hector grumbled as he followed Jack topside.

The throbbing was louder when the two climbed up on deck. They listened for a second.

"That's an engine," Hector said. "Off to the starboard."

The sound cut out. Peering into the darkness, Jack seemed to see a darker mass moving against the blackness of the night, not more than 100 yards off from the *Enigma*.

"It's another boat," Jack said. Without really understanding why, he took the rifles and put them out of sight behind the cabin roof.

A brilliant white circle of light blasted Jack and Hector. They held up their hands in front of their eyes to shield them from the spotlight's glare.

"What do you want?" Hector shouted.

"Be not afraid! Be not afraid!" Vanderlet's voice came back over water, sounding tomb-like as he spoke through a megaphone. "I am come to speak with you a little word."

"Do we have a choice?" Jack yelled back.

"Nee, you do not. Mine regrets. Stay in the light."

The metallic click of a rifle bolt being pulled back echoed across the water. The other boat's lights snapped on. She was a steam-powered yacht, smoke drifting from the amidship funnel. There were also two spars, fore and aft. The name on her bow read *Antoinette*. About a dozen crew lined the railing. Jack easily picking out Swayne's diminutive silhouette.

A launch appeared from around the yacht's bow, accompanied by the purr of its electric engine. As it crossed into the spotlight, the fat figure of Hans Vanderlet standing in the bow came into view. Santley, still in a frock coat and silk hat, sat in the stern, guiding the launch's rudder.

"Don't let them see the rifles," Jack said out the corner of his mouth. Hector nodded slightly.

The launch pulled up the *Enigma's* side. Hector rushed over to grab the painter tossed up by Vanderlet. Jack strolled over to the railing, the spotlight following him as if he was an actor on stage.

"May I come aboard with my friend, der Honorable Santley? I am a man of peace, and I speak with you most fair," Vanderlet said.

"Vanderelt, you constantly turn up like a bad penny," began Jack, "you hypocritical old scoundrel ..."

"There, there," cooed Vanderlet, sighing, "it is mine fate do be always misjudged. It give me pain, but it is so. And mine heart is so kind, it not let me hurt a fly."

"Let them come aboard," Hector said. "We have no options."

"As you like," grumbled Jack. "You both may come up."

"Thanks, thanks," said Vanderlet. "I love to deal with gentlemen. We have your word that we go free when we have talked?"

Jack gave a sharp, sarcastic laugh. "Like previously on the *Etruria?* Certainly you have my word, so we long as you don't try to roast us like a couple of sides of beef."

"Ach, I love a man that can smile of the past."

Vanderlet came puffing on deck, followed lazily by the dandy. Jack took a few steps backward, so Vanderlet and Santley stood between him and Hector.

"I come to make terms," Vanderlet said. "You have a pretty little boat, a pretty boat, Mr. Drayton."

"Never mind the boat," said Jack tartly, "but get to business."

"Ach, yes, yes," Vanderlet's little eyes were watching Jack furtively, "that is so. It is too pretty a boat to spoil. I come as a friend, and I come in peace. It seems we are all after the treasure of Black Juan. We have also a ship, as you can see, and we could eat you up. But it would go to mine heart to fight and to shed blood. Let us be friends. There is money enough for all. Let us not fight, but join company, find the wealth and share with each other."

Jack was quiet for a moment. "That's not a bad idea, you thieving old rogue."

"If he called me that, Hans," drawled Santley, "I'd brain him."

"Silence, fool," hissed Vanderlet.

"Oh, you would brain me, would you?" asked Jack.

"Bai jove, I would," answered Santley, with a yawn.

"You are a miserable rascal and a disreputable cutthroat," Jack replied calmly. "Keep your tongue tight, Santley."

There was an oath, and the dandy's revolver was out. Hector's left arm wrapped around Santley's throat, throttling him. With his right hand, Hector disarmed Santley, and tossed the revolver to Jack. Jack caught it midair, and pointed it at Vanderlet.

"Make sure you know who's behind you, Santley," Hector whispered into Santley's ear. He dragged Santley to the railing and pushed him over. Derisive laughter echoed from the yacht. "Man overboard," Hector announced in a bored voice as he brushed off his hands. Vanderlet returned his gaze to Jack and smiled as if nothing had happened.

"Now, Herr Vanderlet of Schiedam fame," Jack said, "I think you are a sensible man."

"That is so, that is so."

"You want to make terms. As you are a rascal of the deepest dye, I cannot trust you. Therefore, there will be no terms. We are going to Peril Island, so stop us if you can. Get the treasure if you can."

Vanderlet was still smiling. "Mr. Drayton, you are young, smart, brave and resourceful. People trust you."

"Thank you for the compliment. What is this leading to?"

"You know my plan. I make you my London agent. In charge of the whole city. Mr. Dane can help."

"I am sure I speak for Hector. We decline your offer. Now kindly remove yourself." Jack gestured toward the launch.

"You can leave on your own, or Hector can assist you off if you wish."

"It is sad to have to kill you," he sighed. "But it must be, it must be. Mr. Drayton, Mr. Dane, think it over before it is too late."

"There is nothing to think about," Jack said.

"I go, I go," said Vanderlet, shaking his head. "I tell you this: when once I get you, I will make you go on your bent knee to ask pardon for this night's work. You shall hang, and the seagulls shall pick out your eyes. Good night, good night."

He bowed.

"Hurry up," Jack said. "My foot is itching to kick you."

Vanderlet looked Jack in the eye with savage hatred. "One day I shall remember that, and you will have no feet to kick with."

He calmly lit a cigar and waddled toward the railing, slowly climbing into the launch. Santley had already climbed in, and sat, wet and miserable, at his position in the stern. The launch's motor started, and pulled away from the *Enigma*. Vanderlet stood and waved his cigar over his head.

"Good night," he called. "Perhaps we shall meet later on."

He threw the cigar into the ocean with a deliberate motion.

"That's a signal!" screamed Hector.

Gunfire erupted from the yacht. The pitching and rolling of both vessels made accurate aiming difficult, and the bullets sprayed in seemingly random directions, splintering the deck and singing overhead. Jack dove behind the cabin roof. He still had the pistol, and he emptied it in the direction of the spotlight, finally knocking it out with the sound of shattering glass and a shower of flying sparks.

In the darkness, he flipped the crate off the carronade. He touched off the cannon, and it roared a flame of blue-white. A few seconds later, he heard it strike the yacht and shed its flame with a crash.

Jack shouted with triumph and exhilaration. He scrambled around to the front of the carronade and reloaded it. He fired it a second time. The top half of the *Antoinette's* front mast tilted, hung for a second, then with a splintering crack, crashed to the deck.

The *Antoinette* was in chaos, a floating madhouse crowded with raving lunatics, all yelling instructions to each other but nobody listening. An explosion shook her, and flames appeared.

Jack grabbed a rifle and started raking the *Antoinette* with fire. When the first rifle was empty, he did the same with the second. He reloaded both rifles, his fingers working on their own without his conscious effort. He sprayed the *Antoinette* with bullets from both guns, laughing.

He was enjoying himself.

All had happened in a minute. The *Antoinette* was in difficulty. She started going astern at high speed, as if she had had her fill of fighting.

"Ha! They did not expect that, now did they, Hector?" Jack yelled. "Did they, Hector? Hector?"

Jack looked to his left. Hector was sprawled motionless on the deck.

CHAPTER TWELVE

he *Antoinette* steamed astern, the smoke from her funnel mixing with smoke from a fire below decks. Jack decided if the *Antoinette* was sailing in one direction, he'd better sail in the opposite direction.

He ran to the *Enigma's* bow, jumping over Hector's body without so much as a glance. He hauled in the sea anchor and set the fore sail. Rushing to the stern, he set the aft sail. He squatted on the deck to make himself a smaller target in case somebody on the Antoinette decided to take a shot at him again. He grabbed onto the tiller.

"Come on, old girl, catch the wind, you can do it," he urged the *Enigma* as he patted her deck with his free hand.

The sails snapped, then hugged the night breeze. Jack found the north star, steered in its direction, then tied down the tiller. He rushed down to the cabin, vaulting down the companionway. He grabbed the small metal box containing the medical supplies.

Suddenly all the bravado he displayed to Vanderlet, all the energy which had crackled through his body during the battle and the aftermath evaporated. His knees buckled, and he caught the edge of the top bunk to stop himself from collapsing to the deck. He never had felt so tired and so drained in his life. He lay his face on the blanket.

"Hector," he mumbled into the blanket. "I must see about Hector."

He pushed himself back into a standing position with great effort. He found a lantern, and lit it with a trembling hand. Scooping up the metal box and the lantern, he stumbled back on deck.

He walked toward Hector's body, dreading what he could possibly see. He started mumbling the instructions about wound care Agnes had told him to distract him from what he hoped he wouldn't find.

When he reached Hector, he held the lantern over him. Hector moaned, and stirred a little. Jack broke into a relieved grin. As he knelt on Hector's left, he saw an angry gash slashing its way from just above Hector's left eye to above his left ear. Jack opened the tin, pulled out a bottle and soaked a cloth with some alcohol. He started to clean the wound.

Hector sat bolt upright. "Ow! What are you doing? Trying to kill me?"

Jack pushed him back down. He continued his work. "Don't be such a baby. You'd think you've never been grazed by a bullet before."

"I have a wire for you: I haven't. Ow!" Hector jerked away.

"Stop moving! I have to sluice this wound!" Jack roughly pulled Hector closer.

"I see absolutely none of Agnes' calming bedside manner has rubbed off on you."

"None whatsoever."

"Evidently," Hector fired back, crossing his arms. "What happened? Where's the *Antoinette*?"

"When did you leave the party?" Jack pulled out a gauze bandage.

"Fairly early, I'm afraid."

Jack quickly filled in Hector with an account of the battle as he bandaged Hector's head. When he finished, Hector was gazing at him in admiration.

"You did all that? Alone? You are a veritable one-man Royal Navy!" Hector said.

"It must be in my blood. Grandfather would have been proud."

"Well done, old chap!"

"So what do think of my plaything now?"

"I want one for Christmas." Hector sat up, wincing. He looked at Jack. "Do you remember our agreement we made before we set sail, Jack?"

"Yes."

"I'll give you back your promises still," Hector said quietly.

"Do you want them?" Jack busied himself returning the medical supplies to the box.

"I'm hanged if I'll take mine, Jack, but there's bound to be more fun and joy ahead," Hector paused for a second. "What's your opinion?"

Jack methodically returned the bottle of alcohol to the box and snapped shut the lid. He looked Hector directly in the eye. "I'd risk anything to keep the hands of those brutes off the treasure. I'm going to hang on for all I'm worth."

Hector grinned and nodded. Jack stood, and helped Hector to his feet.

"Obviously Vanderlet, Santley, Lake and company must have chartered that boat," Jack said. "How did the locate us?"

"Adding it up," Hector reasoned, "the treasure-seeking syndicate found out we were not killed in the *Etruria* fire. So, they must have kept their eyes on us, or paid others to, even after stealing the parchment. They knew when we left port, and they are, of course, on the same heading as we are. This little meeting may have been simply an accident. After all, coincidences do happen." Hector staggered a little, almost losing his balance. "I still feel a bit dizzy."

"I shouldn't wonder," Jack steadied Hector, then picked up the lantern and medical kit. "I would not be surprised if you will retain a scar from this little incident."

"That will make me appear quite dashing to the ladies, won't it? Should I say it is from a duel of honor, or fighting off dastardly pirates?"

Jack laughed. He handed the lantern and medical kit to Hector. "Either one would work. Try both. I am glad that the head wound has not affected your personality greatly. Now get below and rest. I'll stand watch the rest of the night. You will most likely need to make a course correction tomorrow. Now off with you."

After Hector went below, Jack walked back to the carronade and gave the barrel a couple of affectionate pats. His brain was still excited. He had been in a brisk fight. He had often wondered at the fierce, reckless bravery displayed by troops. Now he understood. There was no time to think or be afraid. It was a kind of madness, a wild desire to get at the foe, an intoxication.

Even though the carronade's surprise element was gone, he replaced the crate over the gun, then sat on it. The overcast was clearing, and the stars gleamed overhead. When he was a steward, Jack frequently headed to the bow late at night, after most of the ship was asleep, to enjoy the solitude and harmony of the calming sounds of the bow breaking the ocean under the magnificent canopy of the heavens. As Jack sat there, that same sense of peace returned, and the evening's occurrences seemed to have happened years ago.

A line spoken by Julius Caesar from Shakespeare's play came to his mind.

"'It is not in the Stars to hold our Destiny but in ourselves'," he said aloud.

The dawn's light was just tinting the sky when Hector tapped him on the shoulder.

"I see you're up and about," Jack said, hopping off the crate. "How's the head?"

"Top form, admiral," replied Hector. "The soon-to-be Doctor Agnes will have some competition from you."

Jack bowed. "Why, thank you sir."

"I will perform the course correction, and now it is your turn to hit the galley. I will take Eggs Benedict for breakfast."

"That sounds delicious, but you will get whatever I throw together. Hash, most likely."

"I shall never book passage on this liner again," Hector sniffed.

"And now, to say what I wanted to say several times when I was a steward." Jack assumed the upright posture and overly-polite smile of a steward. "Bugger off."

Hector fanned himself as if he was a shocked ancient dowager. "Well, I never!"

"And you probably never will," Jack tossed over his shoulder as he went below.

He made breakfast and brought it up on deck. Each of them took charge of the tiller while the other ate, then Jack went below to do the wash up. After the galley was cleaned, Jack picked up the bowl of soapy water and went topside. As soon as he got on deck he stopped.

"Bah!" he growled as he poured the contents of his bowl overboard, "How that water reeks. It smells like sulfur."

"Filthy," Hector agreed.

"How long has it smelled like this?"

"About ten minutes." Hector motioned Jack over to a rope hanging over the starboard rail. He pulled it up, a wet rag tied to the end. "Feel that, Jack. Here, quickly."

Jack grasped the rag. "It's almost warm! And it feels oily. How do you account for it?"

"Probably a hot springs below, or an underwater volcano," ventured Hector. "This is a volcanic region."

Jack dropped the rag and looked around. It was like the *Enigma* was in a dead sea in the midst of the ocean.The stench became more pronounced. Warm as the water was, it gave off no mist. The *Enigma's* wake looked oily and slimy.

The boat continued on the correct course, but seemed to labor to part the water, like a horse pulling a heavy cart. The day dragged on, the sulfur odor making the air thick and almost visible, until the sun finally began to dive into the sea. Jack noticed something on the horizon. He pointed.

"Hector, is that a ship?"

"The *Antoinette*?"

Jack squinted and shook his head. "It is not the *Antoinette*, unless she grew another mast."

"What ship would sail this ghastly sea?" Hector asked. "It can't be a whaler. The whaler is almost a thing of the past with whales vanishing before the pursuit of man. We must be far out of the track of other vessels."

"Still, that's a ship."

There, low down under the deep purple of the darkening sky and a few stars, the dim outline of cross-trees nicked the gray-blue sky. The wind, which had been up to this point constant and reliable, stopped, and the *Enigma's* sails flapped uselessly.

"She's got the strangest tops I've ever seen on mortal ship," said Hector. "Give me the glass please, Jack."

Jack retrieved the glass and handed it over. Hector scanned the object. His voice grew suddenly hoarse.

"By all eternity," he gasped, "there's never a rag on her or a puff of air, but she's moving."

"Moving!"

Jack snatched the glass. The other ship's spars were swaying to and fro. The water was like glass, like ice.

"By Jupiter," he said, "she's coming up, true enough!"

"What's her rig?" prodded Hector. "Can you give that rig a name?"

A gray cloud moved swiftly across the bow, although clear and bright above them the stars glimmered. The smell of the mist was revolting, almost like death. It felt clammy on their cheeks and was heavy with the smell of sulfur.

Then suddenly the curtain parted. It revealed a spectral ship on a glassy sea, suddenly looming much closer, bearing down on them with increasing speed. It was the ghost of a vessel, with broken cordage and paint-less hull, a ship of a hundred years ago! Her spirit ran between two long wooden horns that decorated her figurehead. In the clear starlight the carved demonic face of the figurehead seemed to glare and grin with hideous malignity. Finally Jack caught a glimpse of her painted name in the glass, and a cry broke from his lips.

"It's the *Satan!*"

Hector grabbed Jack's arm. "She's going to ram us!"

Jack aimed his glass at the bow. There appeared to be a figure standing there, silhouetted behind the rotting railing.

"Gaskara!" Jack gasped. He shoved the glass into Hector's hands then cupped his own around his mouth and shouted at the top of his voice. "Gaskara! It's Drayton! Drayton! Do you hear me? DRAYTON!"

From the *Satan* came the sound of rushing human feet. Naked feet seemed to be pattering over the deck. Hector's voice was a scream.

"Look at the yards! Look at the yards!"

The yards had swayed round, and every rotten rope was taut, as if fifty spectral hands might have been at work. The rotten sea-coffin, a derelict of the past, slowly swung round, revealing the rusted muzzles of a row of guns. She was a three-master and a two-decker, with square ports and tall poop deck. The paint had peeled from her in long strips, making her hull look like the ribs of a skeleton. Her deck-house had gone. Forward, the bulwarks had been ripped out of her. An anchor still dangled at the hawsehole, and the capstan held a few belaying pins still.

As she sailed past within yards of the *Enigma*, her wake rocked the smaller boat violently. Jack dropped to his knees and grabbed the railing. Hector lost his balance, tumbled to the deck and slid into the opposite rail.

Jack stared at the ship's stern, the painted name SATAN seemingly glowing with its own unnatural light. The gray mist reappeared, cloaking everything from view, like the final curtain of a play. The mist slowly dissipated. The *Enigma* resumed to an even keel, the wind filled her sails, and once again she sailed calmly under the starry sky.

Jack slowly climbed to his feet. He didn't want to talk to Hector. They would have to convince themselves awkwardly that they both experienced the identical odd interplay of light, shadow, and waves, which led themselves to believe they saw the exact same phenomena, or they would have to admit they have been visited by a phantom vessel captained by a ghostly pirate. Either would be a difficult admission.

When Jack finally glanced back at Hector, it seemed Hector thought the same way. Without a word, he took up his post at the tiller while Jack went to the bow to stand watch.

The rest of the night and the next day passed without anything strange occurring. The next night, the whole northern sky was aflame with crimson light, a light so vivid that it paled the stars.

"There's a red glow due south, Hector," Jack said as Hector came on deck for his watch. "I've been watching it for an hour or more. I should think it's a volcano. I expect there has been a big eruption, and the glow comes from the lava which hasn't cooled down. It is too steady to come from the crater itself. How does the thing go?"

"'Sight Flame Mountain,'" answered Hector, as he took charge of the tiller, "'and the Great Skull Ice. Bear east with the Great Skull Ice to port.'"

"That's where we may tumble," said Jack. "What is the Skull Ice? I suppose it was some berg that old Juan thought bore some rough resemblance to a human skull. Has it been destroyed, has it melted or broken adrift? It was a deuce of a time ago, Hector, and ice won't keep like granite or marble."

"I've thought of that, sonny. There are other things to go on — the blood water and the floating drift-weed. Doesn't that look like a forest on fire? Doesn't it feel warmer?"

Jack checked the thermometer outside the cabin. It had risen nine degrees. As they watched the red glow, the temperature rose so rapidly that the hoar frost melted, and their jackets had to be discarded.

Hour by hour the glow grew fiercer. And then the puzzling mercury slipped back little by little until it was freezing hard, causing Jack and Hector to don their jackets again The whole ship stood out in the uncanny red glare, every board, every nail, every item on deck, distinct. Jack and Hector looked strangely like imps who sailed a fiery ship on a fiery sea. It was amazingly beautiful, but its splendor inspired awe.

"Hello," said Hector, "is that a cloud?"

A black vapor was blotting out the stars.

"It's more like smoke to me," said Jack. "Jupiter! It's coming at a pace."

The stars were vanishing rapidly under the dense black curtain that was rushing over the sky.

"Smoke it is," cried Jack. "Can't you smell it?"

It beat into their faces, strong, pungent, sulphurous. The glare faded murkily, and a great darkness came. Jack and Hector could not see each other's faces through the mist.

The stars had vanished altogether. Jack and Hector started coughing and spluttering.

"There's no smoke without fire," said Jack, "but where's the fire? Bah! This is blinding and choking. Where are you, Hector?"

"Still here," answered Hector at his elbow. "I feel like a smoked haddock."

"And look it," added Jack. "How long is this going to last?"

A crash like a thunderclap shook the vessel, followed by a deep, incessant swelling roar. They both dove for the tiller.

"Hold fast! Hold fast!" yelled Hector. "Keep her bow pointed into any wave!"

The tiller became a living, fighting thing, with Jack and Hector wrestling with it to keep it under control. It wretched out of Jack's hand, and slammed into Hector's stomach, pinning him to the rail. Muscles straining, grunting with exertion, Jack pulled the tiller back to center as Hector pushed.

Louder came the lash and crash of water. And then the *Enigma* sprang up like a cork on the crest of a wave. A torrent of lukewarm water deluged her from stem to stern. For a moment or two, it was waist-deep, and Jack and Hector clung on for their lives. The horrid darkness added to the terror, as Jack and Hector gasped and fought for breath in the stifling smoke.

The turmoil was deafening. Then, shaking herself like some big dog, the gallant lugger shot down the black slope, and another terrible sea struck her. Jack lost his grip on the tiller as another wave swamped the deck. The wave receded, pulling Jack with it. He felt himself hit the railing. He clutched wildly for it as he went over the side.

He flailed about in the angry water. His waterlogged clothes starting to pull him under. He managed to shrug off his jacket as another swell pushed him to the surface. Jack thrashed about madly.

He barely spotted the *Enigma* through the smoke, running up another wave. Jack desperately swam for her, the ocean clawing at him for its possession. As the *Enigma* crested the wave, Jack was pulled underwater again, in a swirling mass of dancing bubbles that seemed to be tentacles wrapping around him. He kicked his way to the surface.

He surfaced in calm water. The clamor and roar were magically behind him, but he was treading water alone. He couldn't see the *Enigma* through the dark and smoke. Panic overtook him momentarily, as he desperately searched around him.

"Hector! Hector!" he shouted.

Silence. Jack yelled again.

"Jack!" Hector's voice reached him through the darkness.

In the darkness and smoke, Jack grew disoriented. Hector's voice seemed to come from nowhere and everywhere.

"Where are you? I can't see you!" Jack shouted.

"The lantern! Look for the lantern!" Hector called out. "Can you see the lantern?"

Jack again scanned the area around him, and with relief, finally spotted a pinpoint of light glimmering through the smoke.

"Yes, I see it! Keep talking!" He started swimming toward the light.

"Keep coming, Jack! You can do it! I know you can do it! Keep coming!"

Hector kept talking, singing, and encouraging Jack as he plowed his way forward through the water, the light grew larger, and Hector's voice became louder. Finally, in front of him, Jack saw the silhouette of the *Enigma* materializing out of the darkness, riding again on an even keel.

Jack's strength began to fail. His strokes became weaker, uncoordinated.

"Hector, I can't reach you!"

"Jack, you can! I can see you! It's just a short distance more!"

Suddenly, Jack seemed to forget how to swim. He splashed and thrashed around in the water, finding it harder to keep his head above the surface.

A rope splashed in the water nearby. Jack made a snatch for it, but couldn't reach it.

"Again!" Jack shouted.

The rope withdrew, then hit the water just in front of him. Jack swam to the rope with the last drop of his energy and grabbed it.

"Haul in!" Jack yelled.

He felt the rope go taut and start pulling him toward the *Enigma*. At the same time, Jack dragged himself along the rope hand over hand, kicking his feet, until he collided with the *Enigma's* hull. Hector reached over and yanked him onto deck like a landed fish.

Jack laid prone on the deck, gagging, coughing, and spitting up water. Hector was on one knee next to him, his two hands pressing on Jack's back, as though trying to transfer some of his life force to him. After some minutes, his breathing returned to normal.

"Permission to come aboard," Jack gasped out.

"Permission granted," Hector laughed, patting Jack on the back.

"Thanks," Jack sucked in air. "That's what it must be like to be keelhauled. That was a little wrinkle Gaskara neglected to tell us about."

Hector helped Jack to his feet and guided him to the companionway. "Get below and change out of those wet clothes immediately."

"Aye, aye, sir."

Jack slogged down to the cabin, and peeled off the wet clothes. After he dried himself and changed into warm clothes, he felt more like a human again than an amphibian. He climbed back on deck.

"I feel much better now. It's your turn, Hector —" Jack stopped.

Hector stood at the tiller, mouth open, staring at something off the bow. He pointed. "Look!"

Jack turned around and gasped. "It's like something out of Dante's *Inferno*."

Through the smoke a streak of vivid crimson light shot across the dark sea. It rested on a lowering object.

A vast skull of crimson, a grisly monument that might have been carved by human hands. The thing was almost perfect except for the lower jaw. It burned like a skull of red-hot steel.

"The Great Skull Ice," said Jack hoarsely.

Slowly the red beam died away, and the stifling smoke lifted. The stars burned in the black arch of heaven. Like a white ghost, the object loomed out of the night.

"That's the most uncanny thing I've seen for some time," Hector said.

The weird Skull Ice and the glow of the Flame Mountain tinged the sky in blood-red to mark the path to Peril Island. They were at the very gates of the Land of Treasure.

CHAPTER THIRTEEN

It was a bitter morning, though clear. The sun was without warmth. In the daylight the curious berg was far less like a human skull. It was a rugged mass of crystal some two hundred and fifty feet high. The volcano was not impressive, but a mere hill rising sheer from the water with a plume of gray smoke above it.

The *Enigma* left the dead sea and entered broken water. The dancing wavelets, silvered by the pale, low sun, were cheerfully welcomed. The rest of the day passed uneventfully.

Down in the cabin late that afternoon, Jack plotted the ship's last coordinates on the chart. He put down the pencil and examined his work with pride. He fancied he was getting quite good at this, especially since he began with no knowledge about charts or navigation. He then finished the ship's log entry. As he rolled up the chart, Hector called to him loudly.

Jack sprang up and rushed on deck. His eyes were suddenly dazzled.

The *Enigma* was afloat on a sea of quivering flame. Waves of fire licked her hull. North, south, east, and west the sea shone like molten metal, glowed, flared, burned. And the fierce frost stung his nostrils and numbed his ears.

"The Blood Water," Jack gasped. "The Blood Water!"

There was something ghastly as well as amazingly beautiful in the strange glare. Hector tied a bucket to the end of a rope and pulled up a sample. He plunged his bare arm into a bucket of the fiery water. It came out glowing like burnished copper.

"Speak, Jack. Any ideas?"

"Obviously, it is an astonishing kind of phosphorescence," answered Jack. "Whether it is a plant or animal I cannot tell, but they probably have the power of transmitting the light at will."

Little by little the crimson tint faded from the water. At last it attained its normal color.

"Well," said Jack, "it is all coming true little by little. We have found the Flame Mountain — a bit of a fraud that, Hector, just the same — the Great Skull Ice, and the Blood Water. What comes next?"

"Hark for the Night Thunder."

"What on earth is that?" Jack scanned the skies. "Do we wait for a thunderstorm at night?"

"Trust us to get a pirate with a poetical streak," sighed Hector.

"There's also something about water that runs strong and smokes, eh?"

"Just so," said Hector. "There's also a long ice shore where the walrus dwell."

"That's the only description that sounds the least bit normal," Jack said.

"It's getting pesky dark," observed Jack.

A darkness fell rapidly, almost like a light being switched off in a room. They could barely see each other. The stars were obscured, the ocean was a sea of ink.

"We should heave-to," said Hector. "It's madness to travel a knot."

The atmosphere was warm, heavy, and oppressive. Nature seemed to be topsy-turvey altogether. Jack went to the cabin, then fumbled for the lanterns and lit them. Topside, he gave one to Hector, who went to the aft sail. Jack went to the bow and struck the sail, and then tossed out the sea anchor. The two returned to midships.

There was a ripple on the water, and the waves beat against the hull, otherwise it was very silent. Solid walls of inky darkness shut them in.

"Gently," said Hector. "Keep your enormous feet quiet, Jack. I heard something then."

"That's what comes from having ears as big as my feet," returned Jack.

"Do shut up, Jack. Listen."

A faint, deep roaring trembled and vibrated through the darkness.

"Maybe there's a wind coming up," said Jack quickly. "We're going to get it hot."

The sound shivered and trembled incessantly. It did not increase in strength. It shivered and quivered and rumbled like distant thunder. The whole air throbbed with the one deep note.

"That's no wind and no surf," said Hector.

"It must be the Night Thunder," said Jack.

"For every cent of Black Juan's treasure, Jack, I'll wager on it. That's what it is. I'd give a hundred pounds for a clear moon. Those are seals raising their sweet songs."

In the morning, the *Enigma* headed for the channel. There was a slight current moving north, and plenty of water. The drift ice was thin and rotten. When Hector relieved Jack on the watch, the open sea was eight knots behind them, and the lugger was keeping a middle course between the stretching snowfields. As the pale and heat-less sun moved to the west, a few bars of cloud swept over it, causing a sort of gray twilight. Gradually the flat shore began to show rows of hummocks that ended in a ridge of cliffs. The channel had narrowed until it was barely half a mile across.

"There are the boys who made the row," said Hector.

"What?" asked Jack.

"The seals, my boy. Look." Hector nodded to the port. "Tens of thousands of them. There's more treasure on those rocks in the shape of sealskin than ever black Juan dreamed of. Good skins are almost worth their weight in gold today. The poor brutes have been pretty well exterminated in most places."

The left shore curved into a wide bay with a broad stretch of smooth yellow sand. Little of the sand could be seen for the black bodies of innumerable seals. Some were in motion; others lay like great slugs. The water, too, boiled with them — battalions, armies of fur seals. Farther back, every ledge of rock had its crowded tenants. They knew no fear. The water around the ship suddenly became alive with black, bobbing heads and glittering eyes, and the air was filled with their hoarse, sharp barks.

The sky had brightened, and the temperature was considerably higher. Jack and Hector pulled off their jackets and gloves.

"The Flame Mountain, the Skull Ice, the Blood Water, and the Night Thunder are all behind us. Are we nearing the floating drift-weed, the next link in the chain that joined Peril Island with the Flame Mountain?" Hector wondered out loud.

"There's a lot of weed about, Hector. We're just passing a regular island of it."

"Hurrah!" yelled Hector.

The channel was choked with masses of green water weed, covered with small flowers of bright yellow. In the slanting rays of the sun, the channel resembled a vast green carpet strewn with newly-minted gold.

"Now we've got a nut to crack," said Hector thoughtfully. "The instructions the old pirate left us warned us to 'mark the drift.' What did he mean by that?"

"Maybe just what he said. Let us mark it and see," said Jack. "There's a patch of clear water over there. We want something we can see plainly."

Hector snapped his fingers and rushed into the cabin, while Jack manned the tiller and maneuvered the *Enigma* to the clear patch of water. Hector returned with Jack's empty suitcase.

"Hold on," protested Jack. "That's my grip!"

"I'll buy you another," Hector replied.

He held it over his head, and launched the suitcase as far as he could. It splashed into the water.

The suitcase danced away, hesitated, turned, and then floated north. Hector followed it with the glass.

"It's coming back inshore," shouted Jack.

"And at a thundering good pace too," added Hector.

Clearly there was a sharp current close to the shore, and its trend was to the south. Near the shore was a streak of open water. The current seemed to gradually become stronger, as the suitcase picked up speed. Hector lost sight of it behind a jutting rock.

"Where is it?" Jack asked.

"I dunno ... behind that rock." Hector scanned the area with the glass. "I don't see any breakers ..."

Jack guided the *Enigma* to a better viewpoint. The suitcase was dancing down a narrow channel that joined the main one at right angles.

"Another mystery explained," cried Hector triumphantly. "Old Black Juan did not leave a great lot to chance. 'Mark Drift' is a good clue. For a fortune, that's the way to Peril Island. We might have easily missed it and have kept straight on."

Jack pointed the *Enigma* in pursuit of the suitcase, getting as close to the shore as he felt he could safely. As they felt the current grab hold of their vessel, they struck the sails. Jack opened his notebook where he had written down the wording of the lost parchment.

"It can't be far now. The white gates are to come, and the current which is strong and smokes. Then there is the long lee shore where the walruses dwell, and a fair wind to the land of treasure. What a 'fair wind' means, I don't fathom."

"It means nothing more or less than plain sailing, I guess," said Hector. "It was the old sailor's way of putting it. Anything easy and simple was a fair wind."

The white gates appeared. Two huge rocks flanked the channel and another provided a roof of sorts, forming a portal through the cliffs. The channel narrowed between the gates.

Jack and Hector remained in awed silence as the *Enigma* entered the gates, as though standing in some great cathedral. Steered by Jack, the small craft cleared the narrows without mishap.

"Could you imagine the seamanship required to guide a ship as large as the *Satan* through this?" asked Hector. He pointed. "Wait! Look!"

Jack saw his suitcase, now traveling in the opposite direction to them. It bobbed along next to the far gate, heading for the open sea.

"It's like two-way traffic on Oxford Street. Strange currents in this area," Jack noted to Hector.

The *Enigma* exited into open water. The white cliffs curved away on both sides, appearing to meet somewhere over the distant horizon.

"Now, my learned friend," said Jack, "how do you account for this?"

Hector looked around. "This is probably a caldera."

"What, pray tell, is that, professor?"

"Pay attention, pupil, for I may seat an examination after. A caldera is the remains of a volcano, in this case a massive one from the far distant past," Hector explained. "After the eruption, the lava was ejected, and the top portion of the cone collapsed, leaving this cauldron-like hollow. The ocean broke through at the white gates, and flooded the area, essentially creating an inland sea."

"I accept the statement," laughed Jack.

Another sudden fall of temperature occurred, and there was a rush for coats and gloves.

"I wish the weather would make up its mind," Hector complained as he pulled on his gloves.

A short distance farther the water seethed with walruses. The huge creatures, with their long tusks and whiskers, swam grunting and calling around the boat. Jack spotted more in the distance, sunning themselves on an ice shelf.

It was growing dark. Wisdom suggested an anchor. Excitement urged them to keep on. Their confidence in Juan Gaskara could not be shaken. Had there been rocks or shoals, he would have written a warning. "A fair wind," as Jack and Hector translated it, meant deep and open water to the shores of the mysterious isle.

The night dragged away, and the faint dawn brought disappointment. Grey waters, unspeckled by any haze that might denote land, enclosed the ship. Two hours later, the two spotted a string of wild ducks were flying south in a long line. They wished they had been some other species, for ducks are powerful fliers. Still their presence denoted land. The glass was brought out.

"Gulls over there," cried Jack.

"Scores, hundreds of them," said Hector, excitedly.

A faint gray patch on the horizon became rapidly darker and less misty. There was a miraculous change in the color of the water. From muddy white it turned to vivid blue. And a sweet scent of spice came on the breeze that kissed their cheeks like scented gossamer.

How slowly the vessel seemed to travel over that azure, enchanted sea. The *Enigma* was gallantly doing her best, but she appeared to crawl. Fish of wondrous colors leaped across her bows pursued by gulls with flashing wings. It was a kind of half-light, reflected by the white cliffs. There was no glare, and the sun more like a hazy moon than the god of the day.

"All this white rock reflects the sun. Maybe that is the reason Gaskara never mentioned missing the sunlight," Jack said.

Slowly the land of mystery began to show itself. A pillar of dull black rose to the east, and jutting-crags began to make themselves apparent. The whole extent of her southern shore was visible in the clear atmosphere. To breathe the air was like drinking wine. It filled their muscles with strength, and warmed the blood in their veins. The closer to the island they came, the warmer the temperature.

Hector rushed to the cabin and brought back the map he had drawn from his memory. The two stared at the map, then at the island, then back to the map, like two tourists on their first trip to a foreign city.

"Bah," Hector grumbled. "I missed some bits."

The island was only perhaps six or seven miles long, and a few wide. The pillar was the dusky smoke of the volcano lying to the extreme east of the island. The volcano rumbled, and belched a ball of black smoke before returning to slumber.

"Clearing its throat," commented Jack.

"No cheap holiday trips here," Hector said. "The island may be on borrowed time."

A ridge of bleak hills rose in the distance. They were the Inky Mountains. The great craggy headland was the Hind Hoof, and islands, really only a small outcropping of rocks, lying near it enclosed the "Cauldron." They gave it wide berth, but they could hear the roar and lash of the seething waves, and see through their glasses the tossing spray smoking steadily. It rose like a great brown and green cone, brown above and green below. More to the east still The Hoof jutted out into the sparkling waters — a great brown strip topped with the softest green.

They headed for Shrapnel Bay, and turned the Hoof. Jack and Hector couldn't stop a cry of delight. The sandy shore of the bay was a whiter than carded wool, and the bottom loomed white under the *Enigma's* keel. Scents, such as no human being, except the long-dead pirates, had ever smelled, poured seaward from the seemingly enchanted island. Great masses of ferns and flowers grew in wild luxuriance beyond the pearly sand, and turtles basked near the water. A streak of shining gold showing over the green back of the Hoof marked the sand hills.

Jack guided the *Enigma* into Shrapnel Bay. The bay was fairly shallow, and Jack maneuvered as close to the beach as he dared without beaching the vessel. Hector released the anchor. There was a splash, a rattle, and a jerk.

They had anchored safe and sound on Peril Island.

CHAPTER FOURTEEN

Peril Island was a little world in itself, heated by its own natural fires; a kind of exotic hothouse, filled with luxuriant plants and flowers: a land where there must be a mild winter, regardless of the latitude; a fairy isle set in an azure sea. They could come to no other conclusion. All organic life — animals and plants, at least — requires warmth, light, and moisture. Peril Island had light, but it was a light weak in heat. The warmth must come from subterranean fires. It was a volcanic isle, as the peak fitly named Brimstone Hill by the dead buccaneer, amply proved.

"What's the second half of Black Juan's instructions?" asked Jack.

Hector pulled out his notes, although he really didn't need to refer to them. "'For the treasure, anchor in Shrapnel Bay. Beware shark, his gate, and the Cauldron.'"

"Check, check, and triple check," said Jack. "Proceed, kind sir."

"'To the left of the flagpole on the Hoof. Pull down the stones with care. The hedde points straight at four hundred paces. Dig here, and you shall find, unless the weather have destroyed. If so, your labor is vain.'"

Hector lifted a pair of binoculars and took long look at the cliff. "No flagpole there," he said. "But Juan Gaskara may have meant the Hind Hoof. Isn't that on the eastern end of the island? Then why 'anchor by Shrapnel Bay'?"

"We cannot expect a flagpole to withstand wind, weather, and decay for eighty years or more," answered Jack. "If Gaskara meant on the cliff, we should find traces of the pole choked away under the foliage. If he intended the Hind Hoof, there can be no safe anchorage in Pearl Bay."

The *Enigma* was anchored in shallow water, so Jack unrolled the ratline over the starboard rail. Holding their boots over their heads, he and Hector climbed down the ratline. They waded through the waist-high surf to shore.

"Should we claim the island?" asked Hector with a grin.

"You mean claim in the name of the people, Crown and Empire of Great Britain?" Jack replied. "How about this instead: I claim Peril Island in the name of Jack Drayton and Hector Dane!"

"It should be in the name of Hector Dane and Jack Drayton," Hector grumbled. "At least that's in alphabetical order."

"There's just no pleasing some people," Jack laughed.

They sat on the ground to put on their boots. Jack held his hand on the dirt.

"The ground's warm," he said. "It's radiating heat. That volcano must be acting like a furnace in a central heating system."

Jack stood up. "Which way? Shall we climb the Horn?"

"No," said Hector as he also stood. "Let's go straight north."

"North?"

"North, of course. We're south of the north pole, aren't we? Let's tour the island and get a better lay of the land.

We'll let the Horn alone for a bit," he added, "and make for Satan's Eye."

After struggling through a belt of grand ferns and prickly brambles, they emerged upon a slope of velvety grass, as brilliant, clear, and soft as the lawn of any English garden. A little further on they came to the edge of a pool.

"The lake," said Hector.

Its blue water twinkled through the stems of a clump of giant trees. It was fringed with palms and great reeds. They stood entranced at the magical picture.

"Never had a place been so miscalled," said Jack. "The name Satan's Eye is an insult and libel."

"Name it, then."

"Fairy Water," suggested Jack.

Hector made a face. "Too poetical. Let's have a dip for a start, and christen it afterwards. I don't think I ever saw anything so beautiful."

The lake's water was as warm as a bath. After an hour, they reluctantly decided to resume their survey. As they climbed out of the water, something scuttled away along the ground and under a bush.

"What was that?" Jack asked.

Hector shrugged. He picked up a stick and poked at the bush. He jumped back with a half-scream.

A monstrous, hairy crab popped out from under the bush. It was the most repulsive-looking thing they had ever seen, more like a gigantic, horny-shelled spider than a crab. The red eyes, as big as six-pences, were fixed in eye-stalks almost a yard long. The shell was speckled with yellow blotches, and the notched claws were broader than Jack's hand. The thing raced back to the waters of the lake.

"It looked a little like a crab. I wonder what it tastes like?" asked Hector.

"Most likely as disgusting as it appears," answered Jack.

"Wait, Jack, look over here!" Hector was checking the area just behind the bush.

"You didn't find anything more ugly than that creature, did you?" Jack came to Hector's side.

"These rocks look like they were arranged here." Hector pointed to a circle of rocks on the ground. He poked his stick through the dirt in the middle of the ring and stirred. Some burned chunks of wood appeared. "This could have been a fire ring."

"Recent?"

Hector shook his head. "I don't think so."

They were at the edge of a dense forest. The trees were a species of fir with tall, red stems, and feathery branches. Jack noticed something and walked over to a pair of trees.

"Hector, take a look at this. It seems to be a hut."

The two trees formed the front corners. Whatever structure had filled in the gap in between had collapsed, but the remaining three walls remained mostly intact. They were made of logs and large branches, with the gaps filled in with mud and smaller branches. The roof, also made of branches and logs, sheltered the interior.

"Gaskara must have built this," Jack said as he stepped inside the hut's dark interior. "He was on this island for years, he said."

"It is substantial, I'll say that. Not as elaborate as the Swiss Family Robinson, but still," added Hector. "It looks like something a sea captain would build."

Jack's foot hit something in the leaves carpeting the floor. He reached down and picked up a rusty ax. "And here's how he did it."

The two poked around the hut, but found nothing but a few pieces of unidentifiable, rusty metal. They continued into the forest, sinking ankle-deep into pine needles and cones as they walked through the depths of the woods. They emerged in a clearing between the sand hills to the south, and the Inky Mountains to the north. The mountains were mounds of shiny, black, volcanic rock.

"Gaskara gave those mountains the correct name," Hector observed.

The two continued east, picking up a small river. They followed its course until it emptied into the narrow but shallow Pearl Bay. East of the bay a swampy marsh took up the entire end of the island, with the volcano Brimstone Hill rising at the very eastern tip like a lighthouse. The Hind Hoof, covered with grass, jutted out into the ocean.

They headed west, passing through a narrow strip of land between a cane break and the bluffs overlooking the Cauldron. They walked to the edge of the bluffs, looking down the short drop to the churning waters that roared like an ancient deity demanding a sacrifice. After a few minutes, they went to the lone tree breaking through the dirt.

"Do you think Gaskara meant this tree as the flagpole?" suggested Hector. "It certainly resembles one."

Jack shook his head. "I doubt it. To the left, or right, or anywhere around that tree is just dirt. No stones, just dirt."

They headed on, and passed an oval rock jutting out of the earth.

"It looks like a tombstone," Hector remarked.

"There's something on it, maybe carved on it," Jack noticed. "Those lines don't seem natural."

They walked up to the boulder and examined it. Carved on it, almost as fresh and clear as when the long-dead hand had scrapped it into the rock, was the ghastly picture of a man hanging on the gallows. Below was scrawled *May Black John hang like this. This is the wish of Seth Lake.*"

Jack and Hector stared at the drawing in silence. It was both a memorial and a curse. After a second, they turned their backs on it. A short walk past the Sand Hills brought them to the Hoof. They looked around.

"Am I getting hot or getting cold?" cried out Hector, pretending to play the child's game.

"Don't be a chump," said Jack. "Spread out and look for the remains of a flagpole."

They scattered in different directions. The ground was choked with dank grass, thorny brambles, spiked cactus, spinifex, gorse, and vines. Both picked up sticks, and they began to pull aside the undergrowth. Up and down they went, nosing and ferreting, but all without result.

"Old Juan's flagpole could not have decayed sufficiently to leave absolutely no trace behind. His instructions were, to 'Pull down the stones with care.'" Hector threw down his stick in frustration. "Where are the stones? There is not the slightest vestige of them, not so much as a pebble."

Jack was certain there was no mistake. The instructions were definite, brief, and plain, and plainer still for Hector's method of remembering them. "Give us the instructions again."

Hector used his fingers to count them off. "One: Anchor in Shrapnel Bay. Two: Beware Shark, his Gate, and the Cauldron. Three: To the left flagpole on Hoof. Four: Pull down stones with care. Five: Hedde — spelled H-E-D-D-E, whatever that means — points straight at four hundred paces. Six: Dig here." Hector spread his arms wide in frustration. "But the essential clues to the discovery of the treasure are lacking, namely one flagpole and one pile of stones."

"Don't give it up, old boy," said Jack. "Let's beat about again."

They started another circuit, during which Jack's bootlace became untied. He dropped to one knee to retie it.

"The cliff."

The words were whispered in Jack's ear. They sounded breathy and as though they came from a great distance, but he definitely didn't imagine them.

Jack stood up and looked around for the source. It wasn't Hector; he was on the far edge of the Hoof, poking around the brush. Jack walked until he stood on the very brink of the cliff. A gull came dappling along below him, and rested on something. It was not on the cliff or on a jutting crag, for he could see the clear water below. Jack got on his stomach and peered over the edge. The gull had perched on a broken pole that jutted outwards from the cliff, forty feet below.

"Hector!" Jack called out. "Found it!"

In a second Hector was on the ground next to him.

"We've assumed it was a vertical flagpole," Jack said as he pointed. "There are also horizontal flagpoles, like the ones on the fronts of buildings."

"Could it have fallen down there by accident? By a storm, or a slippage of the bluff?"

"There is only one way to find out. We have to get a rope. One of us must go down." Jack noted Hector's anxious expression. "I will make the trip down, since you've already described me once as a monkey."

Hector fled. Excellent runner as he was he excelled himself, but to the thrilled and excited Jack, he seemed to take about an eternity. He returned, blowing like a porpoise, with a mallet, a coil of rope, and an iron bar.

They drove the iron bar into the ground. The rope was looped at the end. Jack slipped his foot into the rope and, giving it a hitch round the deeply-sunk bar, moved to the edge of the cliff. He looked down, then back as Hector picked up his end of the rope. Jack took a deep breath.

"Any last words for me to take to the lovely Agnes before you plummet over the edge?" Hector asked sweetly.

"Oh, shut up."

"That's not terribly romantic, old chap." Hector dug his heels into the ground, grasped the rope tightly, then nodded to Jack. "Right, over you go."

Jack backed off the edge of the cliff as Hector began to pay out. Jack swung downwards. He scrambled to find any footholds or handholds in the rocks. Finally he was dangling beside the broken pole.

"Steady!" he shouted.

The rope suddenly dropped a foot.

"That is not what 'steady' means!" Jack yelled.

"Sorry! Rope slipped!"

Jack examined the pole. It had been carefully set into the cliff, supported by wooden stays and broad strips of lead. Half of it had been torn away either by a gale or a fall of stones from above. Its jagged end pointed along a narrow ledge of rock. The path was lost behind a jutting spur.

"Well? Jack?" Hector's voice came from above.

"It has been put here! It's not an accident!"

Jack pulled himself inwards by clutching the pole, and gained the ledge. As cool and thoughtful as ever, he made the rope fast.

"I've tied off the rope to the pole!" Jack shouted. "I'm moving to the left!"

"Understood!"

"To the left of flagpole on Hoof," Jack muttered. "To the left it is."

Jack moved cautiously along the ledge. A slip would have hurled him down, a lifeless and shapeless mass, on the jagged rocks two hundred feet below.

The stones were what he wanted next. Slowly and carefully he moved round the crag, trying to avoid the eggs of seabirds and their fat youngsters. The old birds wheeled around him, shrieking, and chattering with anger and dismay.

"Sorry, sorry," Jack said to the birds, "just passing through."

The ledge grew wider and climbed upwards.

"Hector! Hector!"

In a second, Hector's head popped over the edge of the cliff above Jack.

Jack pointed to his left. "This ledge may lead to the top."

Hector nodded and he disappeared behind the rim. Jack kept on examining each cliff and cranny.

Then he halted. The cliff formed a shallow arch, and he saw something unusual. The crevices here and there supported a few scant lichens and rock weeds. Under this arch, however, a mass of luxuriant ferns grew, and water splashed down steadily from above. Where did the ferns find root hold? It could not be solid rock. Jack whipped out his hunting knife and drove in the blade.

It sank almost haft-deep, and he heard the steel ring against something hard.

The next moment, Jack wrought havoc with the ferns. He flung the plants right and left, and tore up the soil with his naked hands. Then he dropped on his knees, and began to prod and dig madly with his knife. There were crevices everywhere. He had found the stones to the left of the flagpole!

He enthusiastically dragged out the first great boulder, and sent it crashing down. Another followed, another, and another. Hector rounded the corner.

"There's a path of a sort from the top. It was overgrown. I must say it's a much easier —" Hector caught sight of Jack. "Jack, stop, stop! You'll ruin us. 'Pull them down with care.' Don't you remember the instructions? 'Pull them down *with care.*' You're like a bull at a gate."

"You're right. It's the gold-fever," sighed Jack. "I'm awfully sorry, Hector. I hope to goodness I haven't spoiled it."

One by one the stones were lifted down, scraped, dusted with handkerchiefs, and carefully examined for any sign or clue. They were just as carefully stacked. Little by little the opening grew, and the light penetrated a short distance into a cavern.

Their hands were trembling and their muscles ached when only the bottom row of stones remained. Both stripped to the waist during their hot toil, and they glistened with perspiration. Unless Jack had bungled, the secret must be hidden there. They panted like men who had run a long and trying race. The fifth stone was removed, the sixth, seventh, eighth, ninth.

Nothing!

Only one remained.

"Pick it up," said Jack, hoarsely.

"You," said Hector. "I'm — I'm too shaky."

Jack knelt down, and worked his fingers under the stone. It was a very heavy one. He worked it, to and fro to loosen it, and then tugged it out. A shout came from Hector. A snuff-box lay in the cavity, and he made a clutch at it, but Jack had him by the throat.

"Don't touch it! Don't touch!" screamed Jack. "If you move it an eighth of an inch we'll lose all!"

He relaxed his grip. Hector leaned against the cliff, and wiped his face. Holding the box firmly down in its original position, Jack opened the lid. The box contained a single coin — a George III guinea.

The head was uppermost, the face looking straight into the interior of the cave. And Jack understood now what Juan Gaskara meant when he wrote: *Hedde points straight at four hundred paces.*

"I know what it means!" said Jack. "H-E-D-D-E is archaic spelling, or merely poor spelling, for 'h-e-a-d.' The head points straight at four hundred paces. There it is, and what it means."

"I don't see it, Jack," said Hector, massaging his throat. "Dash you, how you squeezed me. Though I felt it, I don't see it."

"I do. We must draw a straight line from Old George's eye. Fancy if we had moved it! By Jove, we might have dug round half circle!" Jack counted off with his fingers. "We want lamps, a tape measure and some tools."

Hector glanced up at the sky. "We're losing the light. We have to continue tomorrow."

"I suppose you are right." Jack sighed with disappointment. He pressed the box more firmly into its place. "Until tomorrow, your highness."

CHAPTER FIFTEEN

J ack and Hector dropped their tools in front of the cave early the next morning.

"Thirty inches is a pace," Jack calculated, "so four hundred paces must be eight hundred feet and four hundred half feet, which makes a thousand altogether."

Hector applauded Jack's math.

"And if you keep after your sums, my lad, maybe one day you will be as smart as I," Jack said.

"That is my life's dream, sir."

"I said maybe you'll be as smart, but do not expect the impossible." Jack laid down flat, and stuck a match into the soil in line with the eye of the coin. It was a doubtful measurement, so he placed the match on its side, and forced a pin into it. He felt confident that he was on the right track. It was impossible to interpret Old Black Juan's instructions any other way. To permit of a direct line of a thousand feet, the cave, into whose dark recesses they were peering, must be very spacious.

"Ready?" Jack stood up and lit the lantern.

Hector nodded. He picked up the spade and pick. They plunged into the dark cavern. Then coughing, spluttering, and gasping they reeled back through the opening. The air was foul and stifling and heavy with some noxious gas.

"Beastly," gasped Hector. "We can't go in there, and how are we going to clear it?"

"A fire could soon do it," suggested Jack. "There's plenty of dry lichens about. A fire would soon cause an out draft, and vent the gas outside."

They began to scrape moss from the cliffs. There was no lack of it. It was heaped just inside the cavern, and a match set it crackling and hissing. Very soon the heap burst into flames. More fuel was added until clouds of smoke rolled upwards and poured out seawards. Twenty minutes or more passed, and then Jack leaped over the fire. He went on twenty yards, fifty, a hundred. He could breathe without any difficulty, and he shouted for Hector to follow. The echoes multiplied the shout a hundred times.

A shiny deposit of lime carpeted the floor of the cavern in the heart of the cliff. The lamp only threw a feeble circle of light, but the gleam flashed on stalactites that hung from the roof like silver spears. The chill of the place struck through them, and their footfalls sounded like an army as the echoes flung them back. They arrived at a junction, with another opening veering off to the left.

"Now which way?" Hector asked. "I've read about people getting lost in caves, and never coming out, like in *Tom Sawyer*."

Jack thought for a moment. He handed the lantern to Hector. "Let's ask King George."

Returning to the entrance, Jack stamped out any remaining burning moss and kicked it aside. He laid down again behind the coin and used the match as a gun sight. The lantern glowed to the left of the match.

"Hector, move to your left!" Jack watched the lantern move a few feet then stop. "A little more to your left!"

The lantern moved in line with the match.

"Stop there!" Jack shouted. "Don't move, I'm coming back!"

Jack walked back to Hector, counting his steps. When he reached Hector, he was standing in front of the left opening.

"We're getting closer," Jack said.

They pushed into the depths of the cave as Jack continued to count his paces. He finally stopped.

"That's about 400 paces. It should be somewhere down here," he said, pausing. "Look about."

Holding the lantern low they examined the ground. It was sandy here. Hector moved on a little to the right. He kicked a stone.

"Stand back," he yelled. "There's a hole here."

As Jack extended the lamp, they shuddered. A narrow chasm, filled to the brim with inky darkness, gaped before them. A deep sullen splash rose from its yawning jaws. The stone had reached water.

"That was a close thing," said Jack hoarsely. "You might have been over.'"

"Something stopped me, Jack; something told me it was there. I can't explain the feeling, but I felt the danger. It must have been the instinct that makes a horse balk at a rotten bridge and refuse to take-off from a treacherous bank. I believe that ghastly pit goes clear down to the sea." Hector laughed nervously. "I'm all shaky. When —"

A sound interrupted him. They stood gazing dumbly into the blackness. At first, it was like a soft whistle, but it increased to a hoarse roar, and culminated in a piercing shriek. No such sound as that had greeted their ears before. There was a note of agony in it, unearthly and terrifying. The echoes beat it back and rolled it around the vault again and again. Jack and Hector turned and ran.

They were panting when they reached the light and the open air.

"No treasure for me," said Jack, with a weak laugh. "I'm not going in there again without plenty of glims. Whew! I'm properly funked. In the name of everything fishy, what gave that yell? The ghost of a long-dead pirate?"

"An animal of some kind," said Hector. "Surely."

"Frightened by a sound. Well, aren't we two beauties." Jack looked over the edge of the cliff thoughtfully. "Perhaps it wasn't much after all ... look, there are seals down there. That pit may go all the way to the sea. Those echoes would turn the bark of a seal into the yell of a tiger. You can always lay on it, though, that a man is frightened into fits by what he can't see or understand. We've in rum part of the earth, and it's been an upside-down voyage all through."

"You're right there," put in Hector, "it has."

Jack was thoroughly embarrassed of his fright. Uncanny as the sound was it could only arise from some natural cause. "Ready to find the bogey again or hear his dulcet strains again, my trembling youth? I'll fasten the end of the tape here, and this time measure as we go along."

"Certainly." Hector re-lighted the lantern, shook himself and grinned. He bowed. "After you."

"My, aren't we the brave one?" Jack said as he headed toward the cave entrance.

They plunged back into the darkness. The sunlight faded away, and Hector followed closely, keeping clear of the tape which ran out swiftly from its leather case.

"Nine hundred feet," cried Jack. "Be steady now."

They moved forward warily.

"Stop!"

They were on the very brink of the chasm. Jack bent down to take the measurement.

"Three-hundred and twenty yards or nine-hundred-and-sixty feet," Jack read off. "It's on the other side. Black Juan's treasure lay beyond the ravine. We are almost within a dozen yards of the pirate's gold."

"We were in such a hurry to get out that we left our chattels behind," said Hector with a rueful laugh as he pointed to the dropped pick and spade. "How wide is the gap?"

"Six feet, I should say."

"Less; five at the outside. Take the lantern and hold it high."

Hector handed the lantern to Jack. He backed up a couple steps, ran and bounded across the chasm. Jack passed the pick over, then hung the lantern on the shovel. Hector took them over the other side. Jack jumped over the gap.

The echoes moaned and whispered above and around. Jack struck a match, and lighted a bunch of the moss. It fell slowly into the abyss, blazing up brightly as it sank and touching the rocky sides with crimson. It grew smaller and smaller, and died out in a handful of sparks.

They seemed to have come to the limit of the cave. A jagged, gray-white wall loomed up. Hector swung the pick. The floor was solid rock an inch below the covering of sand. Nothing could be hidden there. They peered about, expecting every instant to discover some iron-bound coffer or great sea-chest, but they peered in vain.

"There are easier things than finding treasure," complained Jack. "I can't see why, after putting it in here, Old Juan should take any trouble to conceal it further. It strikes me he had done enough in that way before."

"Is there any niche in the rock, I wonder?" Hector turned to the right and scrutinized the jagged face of the rocky wall. For an instant his figure disappeared around an outcropping. The light flung his gigantic and distorted shadow across the stalactites of the roof.

"I've found something, Jack!"

Jack floundered in the darkness toward the voice. Hector had entered a niche and was on his knees.

"Look," Hector said, tensely. "It's a lead plate, and there's something on it, hammered with a chisel. Can you read it?"

Jack sank down beside him. A square sheet of lead, strangely like a coffin-plate, lay flush with the rock. A sprinkling of sand had drifted over it, and masses of pale uncanny-shaped fungi grew around. Jack beat the sand away with his cap. There was an inscription on the plate. With the point of his knife, Jack scraped at the letters clean.

"What does it say?" Hector asked.

Jack mumbled the words over to himself once or twice before he fully grasped their meaning, for the letters were ill-formed and clumsy.

"Satan's Pile is here,
It is all mine, and I saved the gallows work to get it
Would give half of it to kill Monkey Swayne
Ship broken adrift and gone
No more drink left"

Something followed that he could not decipher.

"Get that thing off," said Hector, impatiently.

The lead was cemented in, but the cement had cracked and crumbled here and there. Jack worked round the edges with the spade.

"That will do," said Jack, dropping the spade. "Hector, take that end. Gently, gently."

The slab was lifted from its resting-place, and propped against the wall. The cavity was deep and black. Lying on his chest and holding the light at the full length of his arm, Jack peered below. There was a vault.

"Hand me the pick, Hector."

Striking a match, Hector found the pick and placed it in Jack's waiting hand. He hung the lamp on the pick, and lowered if until it rested on the floor of the vault.

"It looks like only about a seven-foot drop or so," Jack said.

Jack climbed over the edge, hung on for a second, then dropped down, followed by Hector. He picked up the lantern.

"It's there!" Hector shouted.

They had found Black Juan's treasure. Seven tough sea-chests, ribbed with rusted iron bars, corded with ropes that looked as if they would crumble at a breath, gaping, time-stained and thick with dust were ranged in a corner of the vault.

But they were not alone. A grim and silent guardian watched over it — a human skeleton.

The horrid thing fascinated Jack. It was kneeling before one of the crumbling chests, its eyeless sockets turned down, and a fleshless lower jaw resting on a bony hand.

"Nobody could have died in such a position," whispered Hector.

"Heavens!" gasped Jack, "he's tied there!"

The bony fingers were bold together by strips of lead wire, and a hoop had been passed over the breast. Fragments of clothing hung to the skeleton. The attitude was gruesome. The skeleton seemed gloating over something — but what?

Jack slowly approached the skeleton, and motioned Hector to follow. He blew away the dust, revealing a heap of tarnished guineas. There were words painted on the wood. Jack bent over and made them out slowly.

"This is ... Santley ... I have not robbed ..." Jack shook his head in frustration, and squinted to read more. "'Not robbed ... share ... treasure ... cut ... enjoy ... curse ... rot ... lack ... uan Gask ... 826'. This is one of Black Juan's grisly jokes. He had given the corpse a share of the gold for which he had perjured his soul."

As Jack turned back to Hector, his foot bumped the chest. The skeleton fell to pieces with a hideous clatter. Jack grunted as the dust rose in a choking cloud, stepping back while waving it away. When the dust settled, Hector pointed to the chest furthest from the pile of bones.

"Perhaps we should start with that one, shall we?" Hector suggested with mock politeness.

Jack grinned a response and lifted the pick. Thud! went the point of the pick under the lid of the first, and the spongy wood split and fell away. There was an inner case of lead. Again the steel point went in, ripping the top sheet apart like tissue paper. They tore it away with their hands. They knelt before the chest, staring in open-mouth amazement at the glittering contents.

"They don't look real. They can't be real," Jack whispered. "They look false, like something you would see in on stage in a pantomime."

It was an odd collection, and the whole coinage of three centuries was there. Moidores and guineas, Spanish doubloons, Eagles and Louis and sequins and dollars, mingled with fat gold chains with fatter seals, battered snuffboxes and patch-boxes, bangles torn from ladies' arms, thick anklets, ponderous watches of ancient make, miniatures in golden frames, sword hilts, candlesticks, crucifixes, scent bottles, toothpicks, snuffers, shoe buckles, gold lace, hat-buckles, richly-chased poidards, from which the blades had been snapped, massive earrings and finger rings, brooches, necklaces, spectacle-rims, buttons, spoons, censers and communion plate — the wealth of a dozen rifled ships and raided villages, glowed and glittered in the great chest.

Uttering a wild laugh, Hector buried his arms elbow-deep in the gleaming white and yellow coins, and let them fall tinkling through his fingers.

"I want to see more!" Hector yelled. He turned to the next chest.

Jack stood, and put a hand on Hector's shoulder. "Then you'll wait. We need to decide how to get it back to the *Enigma*. The treasure is not going anywhere."

"Yes, yes, you're right. I need to get away from this beastly stuff."

They moved toward the opening in the roof.

"Let me give you a boost," said Hector, linking his fingers together.

Jack scrambled into the upper chamber with Hector's help. Hector handed him the lantern and the pick.

"Place it across the opening, and hold it steady," Hector said. He jumped up, grabbed the pick handle, and, using it as a kind of horizontal bar, swung himself over it and gained the cavern above.

"Very well done. You should join a circus," Jack said. "Let's replace the slab. They never leave the bank vault open!"

They replaced the slab, then they faced each other. What they had accomplished suddenly hit them. Both broke into huge grins.

"We did it!" Jack yelled, as jumped up and punched his fist in the air. "We did it!"

Jack and Hector embraced, pounding each other on their backs. They broke apart, laughing, and threw some punches toward each other. They jumped across the crevasse, and soon stood blinking in the sunlight. Jack took a deep breath.

"It's good to be outside in the fresh air again," he said.

"Takes a good breath, mate, because you're goin' back inside," a gruff voice said from behind them.

CHAPTER SIXTEEN

ack and Hector spun around. Behind them stood two men they never had seen before. One was stocky, with long straw-colored hair and beard. He was pointing a revolver. The other man was tall, skinny, with a prominent Adam's apple and a shock of red hair. He held a gleaming knife in his hand.

"Who are you?" Jack asked.

"And, more to the point, where did you come from?" put in Hector.

"Why, we're the magic spirits of this island! Ye heathens have disturbed our rest!" piped up the redhead in squeaky voice.

The two newcomers enjoyed their joke.

"My, we have Tweedledum and Tweedledee," Jack wryly commented.

"With weapons," added Hector.

"Who?" demanded the redhead.

"Nobody you would know," Jack answered. "Although the resemblance is striking."

"Brown and I comes from the *Antoinette*, if you musts know," the one with the beard said.

"We musts. You slowed the *Antoinette* down, but you didn't stop her," Hector said to Jack. Then he spoke to the man. "I didn't see her. Where is she anchored?"

"Nowheres yet," he answered. "Our cap'in and the Dutchman are palaverin' over how to splits up the treasure. Cap'in wants more pay because of the damage to his ship."

"Yer cannon shot almost started a mutiny!" cackled the other. "So the cap'n ain't anchorin' until we gets a bigger cut. So the *Antoinette* is crusin' around the island."

"But Johansen and I thinks, why wait?" boasted Brown. "We spots yer tub anchored in the cove, so we figure we'll get the treasure first, then sail out on your ship. See? We's smart."

"So we swims 'ere to take a little look-see," Johansen said, "while the others are wastin' their time, sittin' on the *Antoinette*."

"It's a pity the sharks weren't hungry," muttered Hector.

Johansen continued, "We looks around, then we spots that iron bar stuck in the ground topside. That be a strange sight, we says to ourselves. So we climbs down the rope."

"See? We's smart," Brown nodded, tapping his head with one finger.

"We sees some footprints in the guano, and track them. Then we spy that pile of rocks, all stacked neat and tidy like, and the moss and ashes scattered about at the cave opening. We figures there's somethin' big in here," Johansen said proudly.

"Twas kind of ye to leave a glim," chortled Brown.

"Then we hear your voices, and sees the lantern light," Johansen said, "and you sounds awful happy. We figures you found the treasure and we'll let ye shows us to it. So we hides and waits."

"See? We's smart?" Brown said.

"Do stop saying than," Jack said.

"Ties their hands." Johansen said to Brown.

Brown pulled a length of rope from his pocket, and cut it half with his knife. He tied Jack and Hector's hands behind them.

"Takes us to the treasure," ordered Johansen. He motioned with his gun. "Brown, the lantern."

Jack and Hector headed back in the cave, with Brown and Johansen falling in step behind them. The lamp flung its rays about and shone upon the snake-like coil of the measuring tape. Brown excitedly rushed up to it.

"Sees? We's right!" said Brown said to Johansen. He noticed the chasm. He pointed at Jack and Hector. "There be a jump. I bet them wanted us to fall in."

"Would you be so kind?" asked Hector.

"Anyone does any fallin' in here, it'll be them. Now jumps to the other side," Johansen commanded Jack and Hector.

Jack and Hector leaped to the far side of the chasm. Brown picked up the lantern and did likewise. Johansen seemed to shrink from the drop at first, but finally joined the others.

The sand was trampled down, so Brown and Johansen quickly found the slab. Brown slowly read what was written there. They said not a word, but their hard, thick breathing roused the whispering echoes of the cave. The slab was lifted.

"Go — go down first," said Brown.

"No," answered Johansen between his teeth. "I can't trust ye."

"Well, send 'em down first then," Brown said, jerking his head toward Jack and Hector, "there maybe a curse. Pirates' gold always has a curse."

"Good thinkin'," Johansen nodded. He directed with the gun. "Go down first."

Jack and Hector sat on the edge of the opening, and jumped down into the vault.

"I'm goin' then," said Brown, taking the wire handle of the lamp between his teeth. "Swear ye won't take no advantage of me, Nick. I've bin a good pal to you. You can't do wi'out me."

"I ain't going to touch you," said Johansen.

He was in the vault as soon as Brown. They shoved Jack and Hector into one corner, then pushed them to the ground.

A wolfish cry broke from them both as Brown and Johansen spotted the treasure. They rushed to the sea chests, chortling and laughing as they gloated over the gold and jewels.

Jack closed his eyes and dropped his head to his chest. He couldn't watch. The sight of Brown and Johansen salivating over the treasure like dogs over fresh meat was too disgusting; the sting of defeat was too bitter. He began to wonder what his life would have been like with Agnes, what things would have been like if he had just thrown away that parchment, and never embarked on this wretched adventure. Loud, arguing voices brought him back to the present.

"Yer robbing me! Yer robbing me!" Brown's voice shrieked.

Jack opened his eyes. Brown and Johansen were standing, toe to toe, weapons in hand, screaming at each other. A legion of fiendish voices flung back their words, smearing them together so much as to make them not understandable.

The argument reached a crescendo of accusations, as the two engaged in a mutual shoving match. Brown whipped up his knife and plunged it deep into Johansen's chest, while at the same time Johansen fired.

Brown's scream rang high and loud above the clamor of the cave. He lurched forward on his face, writhing, then staggered to his knees. His voice cracked in his throat, and he pitched backward to the ground. A convulsion shook his body, and then it was still.

Johansen fell sideways with a dropping jaw, and crashed into the treasure. A red stain spread on his shirt around the knife. His hands reached out, grasping at the air, as though knowing they had to do something but not remembering exactly what, then dropped to his sides. He stared glassily ahead through half-closed eyelids, his lips moving without sound, a pink foam bubbling on his beard. Then, he too, was completely still.

Jack and Hector stared at the scene in shocked silence.

"They were the smart ones. Yes they were," Jack said in a low voice. "I think we've witnessed the treasure's curse in action."

"Jack ... Jack ..." Hector stammered out, "They're dead. They're both dead. They killed each other. I've never seen what a horrible mess a bullet makes of a man ... the blood ... look at all the blood ..."

"Hector ..."

"Jack ... Jack, I think I am going to be sick ..."

"Hector, stop it! You're not going to be sick! We don't have time for that!" Jack commanded. "Just look away. Good. Now put your back against mine. I untied us once, let's see if two's the charm."

Hector scooted around so he sat back-to-back with Jack. Jack picked at the ropes.

"No, they're too tight ... they have to be cut," Jack sighed in frustration. He got an idea. "I'm going the get the knife."

"Jack, no! You can't!"

"Don't look, then!" Jack hissed back.

Jack got up and walked over to Johansen, then sat down with his back to him. He grasped the knife and pulled.

The knife held fast.

Jack wiggled the handle a few times, took a tighter grip, and yanked. With a sickening, moist crunchy sound, like pulling a knife out of a juicy melon, the weapon came free. He maneuvered the blade against the ropes binding his wrists, and started to saw. It only took a few cuts for the blade to slice the ropes. Jack pulled his hands around in front of him. They were covered with Johansen's still warm blood.

"It's a good thing Brown kept his knife sharp," Jack said as he approached Hector. "Here, you're next."

Hector pulled back, eyes wide and mouth open in horror.

"Hector, turn around so I can reach your hands," Jack said irritably.

Hector didn't move, but continued to stare at Jack's hands.

"Hector! Turn around! Now!" Jack barked like an army sergeant.

Hector finally complied, and Jack cut the ropes. Hector faced Jack.

"I'm sorry, Jack. It's just ... I've ... I've never seen a dead body before. Never. It's ..." Hector's voice trailed off. He pointed and shouted. "One moved!"

Jack threw a glance over his shoulder at the bodies. "Neither one moved. It's a trick of the light. The flickering lantern is throwing shadows."

Jack spoke with calm authority. "Hector, look at me, not them. At me. Good. I need your help. Do you think you can help me? I need your help now. Can you?"

Hector took a deep breath, then nodded.

"We have to move them," Jack said.

"Move them? Why?"

"We don't know if Vanderlet and the *Antoinette's* captain have finished their negotiations," Jack explained. "If they did, they will land soon. I'm sure they realize by now that those two deserted. It's not much of a guess that they're on the island and why they came here. Vanderlet and company, plus the *Antoinette's* remaining crew will comb this island to find Brown and Johansen. If they find their bodies, they may call off the search and leave just Vanderlet and the others on shore to find the treasure. I'm sure Vanderlet doesn't want the *Antoinette's* crew tramping all over the place, possibly destroying clues. That may give us enough time to get back to the *Enigma* and set sail." Jack longingly gazed on the treasure and sighed. "Maybe we'll have enough time to take at least some of this with us. Can you help me, Hector? I can't do it alone."

"Yes, yes I can." Hector licked his lips and took a deep breath. He nodded and forced a smile. "Let's get at it."

Jack dragged the two bodies over to below the opening, and boosted Hector to the upper level. Jack hoisted each body up so that Hector could grab the wrists, and then pull the corpse up. When the two deserters were on the top, Jack stuck the gun in his pocket, and gripped the knife in his teeth. Hector helped Jack up.

"Let's pull the slab across the opening," Jack said as he slipped the knife into his back pocket, "then we'll get them across the gap. It may be tricky, but I think we can do it."

After moving the slab, Jack jumped to the far side of the gap. With much stretching and straining, the two bodies were transferred to the other side, then finally taken to the cave entrance.

"Well done," Jack panted, rubbing a bead of sweat off his forehead with the back of one hand. "Now, where's the *Antoinette?*"

"I'll check," Hector answered, and quickly moved up the ledge.

Jack's eye caught the gleam of gold snuff box, still in its original position. He kicked it over the edge of the cliff.

G. W. James

"There, Vanderlet," he said to himself. "Maybe I've made things a little more difficult for you."

Hector returned, slightly out of breath. "She's anchored off the east end of the island. Perhaps Vanderlet didn't want her spotted by us."

"He wanted the element of surprise this time," Jack said. "Let's put Brown and Johansen between here and the Cauldron. Brown first."

They moved the bodies, placing them on their backs. After putting them down, Hector stepped back a distance.

"Now, this needs to look like what happened in the cave happened up here," Jack said. He arranged Brown's body to match how he fell in the cave. Then he went to Johansen, pulling the gun out of his pocket. "Do you remember if Johansen held the gun in his right or left hand?"

"I don't know."

Jack thought for a moment. "Right, I think." He placed the gun in Johansen's hand.

"What about the knife?" Hector asked.

"Why, it has to go back where it came from," Jack matter-of-factually answered.

"Jack! No! You can't!"

Jack responded by plunging the knife into Johansen's chest. He stood, checking his work.

"There, that's a job well done. It wouldn't fool Chevalier Dupin, but it should fool the *Antoinette's* crew." Jack turned to Hector.

Hector was pale, and swaying slightly on his feet. Jack hurriedly went to him, blocking his view of the scene he just arranged.

"Well done, old chap," Jack said, gripping Hector's shoulders. "Very good. I'm proud of you."

"How could you do that? Doesn't it trouble you to be around them? To see them? To touch them?" Hector asked.

"When the carriage overturned, I was pinned under my parents' bodies," Jack explained softly. "I had to crawl over them to escape the wreckage."

"Jack, I didn't know ..."

"Well, it is not the kind of topic which comes up during casual conversation, is it now?" Jack smiled and patted Hector on the back. "Let's get back by the *Enigma*."

The two started for Shrapnel Bay. As they passed the Hoof, Jack diverted to the iron bar.

"Let's get rid of that big signpost," he said.

He and Hector yanked the bar out of the ground and buried it in the sand. Staying low, they skirted the sand hills and plunged into the forest. After a few minutes, Hector held out his arm to stop Jack, then placed his index finger to his mouth.

There were others moving in the forest. The sound of somebody creeping stealthily filtered through the tress. Hector pulled Jack down, behind a bush.

"That could be some of the *Antoinette's* crew," Hector whispered into Jack's ear, "searching for Brown and Johansen. It sounds like they're in the northeast part of the forest, but the sound carries in here, so they could be anywhere. Don't move."

Jack nodded.

The footsteps continued, slowly, furtively, pausing occasionally before resuming. The sound seemed to be nearing Jack and Hector's hiding place. Jack's hands formed into fists, and his muscles tensed.

The rustling grew louder. Jack held his breath.

A pistol shot rang out from the area around the Cauldron, startling Jack so much he almost jumped up.

"They found 'em," a voice said.

"Aye," responded a second voice.

The others quickly walked away from Jack and Hector, crunching through the forest toward the location of the gunshot. The forest grew quiet again. Jack and Hector looked at each other, let out their breaths and grinned. Hector nodded toward Shrapnel Bay.

They jogged through the trees until they reached the edge of the forest overlooking the bay. Crouching down, they checked out the *Enigma*. She floated peacefully at anchor. Not seeing anything amiss, Jack and Hector waded out to the ratlines and climbed aboard.

"It's good to be aboard," Jack said with relief.

Hector nodded. He opened the companionway and went down to the cabin, Jack following.

Lake slouched against the wall, while Santley was comfortably stretched out in one bunk. He raised his pistol toward them.

"Bai jove! It is about time the cubs returned to their den," he greeted.

CHAPTER SEVENTEEN

There was the sound of footsteps on the deck. Jack and Hector looked behind them. Guerin blocked the companionway.

"Oh, this really is too much," Jack said with exasperation. After all the work finding the treasure, after moving the deserters' bodies, after hiding from the *Antoinette's* crew in the forest, Jack returned to the *Enigma* and to this. For some reason, the situation struck him as funny. He began to laugh.

Santley recoiled slightly, as though Jack was contagious with the plague. "I say, the lad's barking mad!"

Jack finally composed himself. "To what do we owe the displeasure of your visit?"

"Vanderlet wishes to see you two," Santley drawled.

"Oh, does he now?" Jack said.

"What if we don't wish it?" asked Hector.

"I'm afraid we have to insist," Santley replied.

Lake opened an ugly knife and felt its razor-like edge with his thumb. He smiled.

Jack bowed. "In that case, we are pleased to accept your gracious invitation."

Santley led the way back into the forest, with Jack and Hector following. Lake and Guerin flanked them.

Hector caught Jack's eye, and nodded his head to his right slightly. Jack nodded, and tilted his head to his left. Hector suddenly dashed off to his right.

Jack bolted to his left and dove into the forest. He ran, dodging trees, pushing away some branches while getting whipped by others. He heard Guerin pounding behind him. He jumped a fallen branch, but slipped on the thick carpet of pine needles. The moments it took him to regain his balance allowed Guerin to catch up.

He tackled Jack, and both smacked into the ground. They thrashed and grappled in the pine needles and dirt, grunting and panting like two wild animals, neither one able to gain the advantage. Finally, Guerin flipped Jack on his stomach, seized his right arm and twisted it painfully behind his back. Jack fruitlessly tried to use his left hand to punch Guerin until Guerin got control of his left arm as well.

Guerin yanked Jack to his feet, both arms locked behind him. He shoved Jack in front of him and returned to Santley. Santley was leaning against a tree, indifferently cleaning his fingernails with a pocket knife. He didn't acknowledge Jack's presence for a moment as he continued working on his fingernails.

Hector reappeared, propped up by Lake. Hector wiped off the blood trickling from one corner of his mouth. Santley, apparently satisfied with the condition of his nails, folded up the pocket knife and slipped it into his pocket.

"This is all well and good!" Santley exclaimed. "We are all back together, as friends should be. Let us proceed to our appointment without further incident."

"Are you all right?" Hector asked.

Jack nodded. "You?"

Hector nodded.

Lake and Guerin pushed Jack and Hector forward with Santley again leading. They walked through the forest without talking, the only noise from the crunching of the pine needles underfoot.

Jack knew he was coming to the end of the adventure. How it would turn out, he didn't know. Something Robert Louis Stevenson wrote came to mind, although he couldn't remember exactly where he read it: *Keep your fears to yourself, but share your courage with others.*

He felt himself standing taller, and walking with a more sure step. Whatever was ahead, whatever the outcome, he could face it. He would not let his anger control him. He glanced at Hector. Hector was looking back at him with the same admiring expression he had on the Enigma when Jack told him about the battle with the Antoinette. Hector gave an approving half-smile and nodded.

The group came to the bluff by the Cauldron and stopped by the tree. Santley gave a perfunctory "wait here" gesture and strolled to the cane break. He disappeared through it, and in a moment returned, holding the cane aside as if holding a door open. Swayne came through first.

Vanderlet followed. He mopped the perspiration from his forehead as he walked and pulled off his slouch hat to Jack. His linen suit and white tie were spotless, his clothes were neatly brushed, and his heavy gold watch chain seemed, like his boots, to have been recently polished. He was smoking a stump of cigar impaled on the blade of a pocket- knife.

"Bah," he said, "it is too hot, far too hot for a man of my size, Mr. Drayton. I fear that I get old. Ach, yes. We cannot be young and strong forever. Have a cigar?"

"I do not smoke. Thanks."

Vanderlet sat down on the sand. "Phew!" he said, "I am not made for this climate." He fanned himself. "Mine dear friends, I know you would be insulted if we did not visit you when we arrive. I can see our welcome shining in your faces."

"Out, with it, Vanderlet," said Jack, bluntly. "Don't fancy you're going to bluff me into giving you time to load up your boat for an invasion. I know those games. It wants something a bit more up-to-date to catch me. Out with it in three words."

"That is so, that is so," answered Vanderlet, "Ach, we were not born yesterday."

"Next?"

"Will you take us to the treasure?" asked Vanderlet.

"As of yet, we have no treasure to take you to," Jack answered. "We have not found it."

"No?"

"No," Hector said, catching on to Jack's intent. "Old Juan's directions are confusing. We have come up a cropper."

"That is too bad," sighed Vanderlet. He looked Jack and Hector over. "Monkey, see what Mr. Dane has in his pocket."

Hector's hand automatically slid down to his pocket. Swayne pushed it out of the way and pulled out a glittering bracelet.

"Where'd ye find this bauble?" sneered Swayne. "Lying in the grass, twas it?"

"I couldn't resist," Hector apologized to Jack.

"My friends," said the honey-sweet voice of Vanderelt, "I have a word to say. I am most kind and good and gentle. I would not strike a dog, but if you try to play me false again, I will tear you to ribbons. We can find the treasure, but taking us to it saves time and effort. And your discovery may have destroyed clues."

Jack thought about kicking the snuff box into the ocean. He smiled and gave a slight shrug. "Perhaps. Perhaps not."

Vanderlet glared at Jack. "Will you take us to the treasure?"

"No," said Jack, "not in this world."

"I agree with Jack," added Hector.

"I do not ask you, Mr. Dane. I do not care for your opinion." Vanderlet continued, sounding disappointed. "Mr. Drayton, that ends it. I try to be nice. I make offers to you of money, of power and position. You take none. I am now done. It come now to dagger's point. I shall hunt you down, kill you and I shall wreck your boat. If you live, I cannot live. When I tell you I am a man of peace I do not lie. I am not when I sleep. Ha, ha, ha! I can do neither while you two live. Therefore, I will kill you and your friend."

"Clear out," said Jack.

"Double," said Hector.

Vanderlet made a slight motion with one hand. Santley pinned Hector's arms behind him, and dragged him to the edge of the bluff.

"I ask again: take me to the treasure," Vanderlet said

Jack and Hector exchanged glances.

"Never," Hector said.

"No," Jack said.

"So brave, so foolish. But the willful man will have his willful way," sighed Vanderlet. He flicked one hand, like waving away a gnat.

"Make sure you know who is behind you, mate," Santley growled. He threw Hector into the Cauldron.

"Hector!" Jack shouted. He fought but Guerin held him fast.

Hector hit the churning water, and immediately was pulled under. He surfaced and the waves tossed him around like a toy. His arms rose and fell in his frantic efforts to escape. The waves pushed him close to where the foaming ocean gushed and roared over the barrier of jagged rocks. The current buffeted Hector to and fro. He swung for a second against the upper edge of the rocks, and then a stronger eddy whirled it over, and crashed down over him, pushing him under. His cap broke the surface, and the waves carried it out to sea.

Hector did not come up again. Then the only motion came from the roiling waves.

"That's ... That's murder!" Jack screamed at Vanderlet. "Murder!"

"It is more simple to talk to only one, Mr. Drayton. Two give each other false courage. I am most gentle. One last time. Take me to the treasure. Agree, and I let you pick your fate," Vanderlet smiled blandly. He spread his arms wide. "I let you live out your life on this lovely island. But too I have a kind heart. I leave a gun here with one bullet in it. If you do not agree, Monkey will make your death long and full of great pain. Now, Mr. Drayton, your answer?"

Jack took a deep breath and pulled himself up to his full height. "Go to blazes."

"Mr. Drayton, you are a terrible man, a real terrible man, and Hans is getting old and fat. I am a man of peace, and old Hans does not wish to see what happens next. It will make me ill. If you change your mind, I may order your death be quick. I wish you a happy afternoon." Vanderlet awkwardly got to his feet and waddled away.

Swayne swaggered up to Jack.

"Aye, something I've waited for, my pretty, waited and prepared for. I owes you a bit, eh?" Swayne pulled a cat-of-nine-tails out from under his coat. "I'll flay you alive, and pour yer own gold down yer lyin' throat. Then I'll cut the treacherous tongue out of ye, ye dirt."

"Swayne, I recall one of our meetings in London," Jack said. "Here's a reminder for you."

He spat in Swayne's face.

Trembling with rage, Swayne wiped the spittle off his face with the back of one hand. "Burn you!" he screamed. "I'll make you suffer for this! Oh, how you will squeal, you long-nosed pig! Not an easy death to die, yers will be! Slow and full of pain!"

Lake came up to Jack, and flashed a hideous shark smile. Guerin grabbed Jack's arms from behind as Lake pulled out his knife. He took hold of Jack's shirt, then cut and ripped it off, stripping him to the waist. Santley moved Lake out of the way and stood in front of Jack.

"You called me 'a miserable rascal and a disreputable cutthroat' the last time we met I believe," Santley said. "I won't have it, I just won't have it. I said I'd brain you, but I do not wish to spoil Monkey's fun."

"Ah, go ahead," Swayne said. "Have at 'im."

"Very obliging of you. Thank you." Santley smiled, then worked Jack over with a flurry of body blows. "Now, will you take us to the treasure?"

"No," Jack gasped out.

Santley slugged Jack with a right cross. "Now?"

Jack spat out some blood. "No."

Santley shrugged. With each one holding an arm, Lake and Guerin dragged Jack to the tree. They pulled Jack face-first to the tree and wrapped his arms around the trunk. Guerin held Jack's wrists, while Lake tied them together.

"On his knees! On his knees!" Swayne ordered. "So he can beg! Beg! I wants to hear the dog plead for mercy!"

Lake pulled out Jack's feet while Guerin pushed down on Jack's shoulders, scraping him down the tree trunk to his

in smothering darkness. He lost all perception of his physical being, seemingly transformed into just a soul floating in empty space.

"Jack?" A voice penetrated the void.

"My mother ... my father ... my uncle," Jack mumbled, "I saw them. They're waiting for me."

"Can you hear me? Jack?" The voice spoke sharply. "Jack!"

It seemed like an eternity before he could muster the energy to answer. "I am Jack."

He felt himself come together like the pieces of a puzzle, reattach, return to a world of sight and sound and sensations. Jack's eyes fluttered open. He was lying on his stomach, facing what looked like a log.

"How do you feel?" asked a familiar voice.

Jack recognized it, and thrashed upright to face the voice. "Hector!"

Hector sat cross-legged in the dirt across from him. They were in Gaskara's hut. Rain pounded on the roof, with rivulets of water running through.

Hector smiled and pointed toward the roof. "Not completely waterproof, but serviceable."

"Hector! It's you! You!" Jack exclaimed. "But it can't be! You're dead! Then I must be dead as well. Are we phantoms, cursed to wander this island for all eternity?"

"Neither of us are phantoms, nor dead yet. I almost surely was, and I must admit you gave me a fright there for a while."

"You were thrown in the Cauldron. What happened? How did you get out? What did you do? How did you survive?" Jack babbled.

"One at a time, one at a time," said Hector, holding up his hands to stop the onslaught of words. "Firstly, how do you feel?"

"I feel right as rain," Jack automatically answered. "Actually, I feel better than that."

Then confusion swamped him. He clamped his hands to the sides of his head, as though to keep it from splitting in two. "No, how could that be? That doesn't make any sense. Not after what I went through ... I mean, was it a dream? Did I hallucinate it? What happened to me, what happened to you?"

Hector shook his head. "It was no dream or hallucination. It all happened."

"You should be dead, but there you sit. How?"

Hector's face seemed to age twenty years. He spoke quietly. "I managed to get my head above the water and grab onto a rock. They say when you are about to die, that your whole life flashes before your eyes. That's just not true. All you can think about, the only thing on your mind, is how to live just a little longer, how to wretch out of death's hand just a few more precious seconds of life. The currents were grabbing at me, dragging me under. I started to lose my grip on the rock. My strength was almost gone. I floated in a gray, liquid limbo, this world slowly fading to nothingness. I began to slip back under the waves, then I found myself on the beach."

"You climbed out?"

Hector opened his mouth, closed it, shook his head then shrugged. "I don't know. I really don't know. I don't remember exactly how it happened. It felt ..." He stopped, as though recalling his experience afresh and searching for the correct words. He took a deep breath before he continued. "It felt as if two cold hands helped me climb out of the water."

"Two hands? Whose two hands?"

"I had the strongest sensation that ..." Hector shook his head in disbelief. "No, it's too mad."

"Any more so than what we've already experienced?"

"No, that's true." Hector took a deep breath again, and spoke as if he was trying to convince himself more than Jack. "I had the strongest impression that Gaskara helped me get out. I don't know. It seems silly. It was just a feeling, but I can't get it out of my head. I didn't see anyone else, but, nevertheless, I was out of the water. So I must have done it somehow on my own, it's the only sensible explanation ... but I just can't shake that other thought. Anyway, I was alone on the beach. I just laid on the sand, exhausted, like a half-drowned rat, vomiting water. I heard what they were doing to you. Swayne's cackling laugh, the snap of the whip, your screams ..."

Hector rubbed his forehead as if trying to scrub the sound from his head. "... the pain, the sheer agony, in those screams." Hector dropped his hands and looked at Jack. The words tumbled over each other. "I couldn't help you. I'm sorry. I was just too weak. I couldn't help you. I'm sorry. I wanted to, but I couldn't ..."

"I understand. I do," Jack said softly. "Then what?"

"After a while, your screams stopped. Swayne and the others left, laughing as if leaving a pub for the night after having a grand old time. Then there was this awful silence. I wondered if you were up there dead, and I would be the only living being on this island. After I regained my strength, I made my way back to you. You were unconscious, and I cut you down. I didn't think it would be wise to return to the *Enigma*, so I carried you here, and washed the blood off your back with the lake water." Hector held up his blood-soaked shirt as evidence. "Mrs. Clare will never get those stains out."

Jack smiled in appreciation of Hector's attempt at humor.

"I watched over you, then I fell asleep. I awoke just before you did, and checked to see how you were doing." Hector spoke like a scientist not believing his own results. "Your wounds are almost healed. They will be in a few days or so."

"Almost healed!"

Hector confirmed with a head nod. "You will only have scars on your back."

"That's impossible," Jack said.

"Yet that is precisely what has occurred," Hector said. "To quote Sherlock Holmes, 'once you eliminate the impossible, whatever remains, no matter how improbable, must be the truth.' The truth is, in a few days, at the most a week, there will be only scars on your back."

A thought started forming in Jack's mind. It was fantastic, outlandish, but it was the simplest, most direct, explanation for what happened. He spoke as he worked out things in his head. "Do you remember removing the stones from the cave entrance?"

"Jack, what does that have to do —"

"Hold on a moment," Jack interrupted. "Do you remember?"

"Yes, of course."

"Do you remember how many there were? How big they were? We cleared all the rocks in one go. Yes, we were tired and sore at the end, but we did it. You're strong because you once shoveled coal in ships' engine rooms. Even so, do you think you could have shifted all those rocks without stopping to rest, at least once?"

Hector shook his head. "No."

"We carried the banner around this island that first day, yet we didn't stop. Yesterday, you carried me here, a distance of at least two miles. Did you rest at all? Stop at all?"

"No."

Jack paused for a second, as the ideas lined up in his head. "Hector, how have you felt since coming to the island?"

"What are you getting at?" Hector cocked his head, puzzled.

"Physically. How have you felt physically since coming to the island? What words would you use to describe how you have physically felt?"

Hector fumbled for words. "Alert, well, healthy ..."

"Stronger?" Jack ventured.

Hector thought for a moment, then nodded. "Yes. Stronger."

"I'm not talking footle here, but I think it is this island," Jack said. "It is the island's atmosphere, or the water, or the fruit on the trees, or fumes from the volcano, or maybe even the dirt itself, something. Somehow the island's natural processes work together, or perhaps a few work together, or maybe it's just one, but the result is just the same: increased vitality. An increase in a person's strength, and stamina. It even speeds up the healing process." He stopped when a final, inevitable conclusion hit him. "These processes could also lengthen a person's lifespan."

"Are you saying that this island grants immortality?" Hector asked.

"No, no, not immortality," Jack answered. "There is death on this island. We've seen it. What happens is that staying on this island increases a person's lifespan."

"Ours? Are we going to live longer simply because we came here?"

"Ours. Gaskara's. Even Swayne's."

"Swayne!" exclaimed Hector. "Are you suggesting that Swayne is over 100 years old?"

"Gaskara was, and he spent years on this island, in this very hut. Swayne also spent time on the island. Do you really want to think that there is a family lineage of Monkey Swaynes running about?"

"No, perish the thought," Hector said with a grim laugh. "If what you say is true, then the island's true value is more than the treasure. It's the health properties. Whatever this mysterious property is, if it could be identified and isolated, it could be a boon for humanity."

"I hate to call a halt your shaping, but I think those properties come at a cost."

"A cost? What do you mean?"

"The cost is insanity." Jack leaned forward. "Gaskara experienced moments of insanity. Swayne is certainly off his onion. Remember the tale written on the linen?"

Hector nodded. "The original Vanderlet lost his mind."

"Do you recall that note I found in the carronade? Gaskara wrote 'harsh mistress.' We didn't know what he meant then, but now I think he meant Peril Island is the harsh mistress. It gives with one hand, then takes with the other. It will give more strength, more life, but extracts sanity as payment."

"What about us, old chap?" Hector asked, concerned. "We have spent time here. Are we doomed to a long life of insanity?"

"I don't know. We have experienced some of the effects already, such as the strength, vitality, and healing," Jack answered. He thought for a moment, puzzling things out. "The effects may be cumulative. How strong and how long they last relate to the length of time on the island, or drinking the water, or eating the fruit from the trees. We've only been here a few days, much less time than Gaskara and the others, and we've been eating food from our stores on the *Enigma*. Maybe a person's initial mental and physical states also affect the outcome. Those pirates who came here certainly were not pillars of strong moral or mental attitudes. But I think we should get off Peril Island as soon as we can."

"Which leaves a big question. Shall we leave with or without the treasure?"

"Hector, we have been beaten, robbed in my own house, tortured, nearly burned alive, and shot at. I've been flogged to within an inch of my life and you nearly drowned. We didn't go through all of that to leave with nothing," Jack said. "Although we have to deal with the *Antoinette*."

Hector smiled. "There, I think, we have advantages."

"We do? How so?"

"They think I'm dead," Hector pointed out, "and that you are either dead, will be dead or, at the very least, still tied to that tree, in no condition to do anything. It's been about maybe eight hours since they left you. Those villains won't be on their guard tonight. They believe they have no reason to be. Not only that, this storm blew in early this morning, and it seems determined to stay through tonight. That also has kept those blackguards on the *Antoinette* all day, who apparently are like cats not liking to get wet. It will also give us cover. Perhaps we can throw a little boarding party when it gets dark."

CHAPTER NINETEEN

The night rain was falling in large, warm drops, when darkness came.

Dressed only in their trousers with knives tucked in their belts, Jack and Hector kicked their way toward the *Antoinette* using a large branch as a float. They didn't speak, but instead focused on their objective with grim determination. The rain fell with a faint, hissing sound. They moved so noiselessly they passed through a cluster of gulls that were dozing on the water without disturbing them.

They neared the launch moored at the *Antoinette's* side. Jack and Hector pushed off the branch and swam the few strokes to the launch. They pulled themselves into it. Jack sucked in his breath and groaned.

"My back's not completely healed," Jack replied in a low voice to Hector's inquisitive look. "The saltwater stings."

"At least you didn't bleed again," Hector said quietly. "It would have attracted the sharks."

"Your concern is heartwarming," Jack whispered back. He gestured toward the ratline. "Shall we?"

"But of course," Hector answered.

They carefully clambered up the ratline and peered onto the deck. It was empty, so they climbed onboard. The velvet darkness baffled Jack's eyesight. He could make out the smoke-stack and smell the hot scent of a banked-up furnace mixed in with the rain's fresh scent. A wind was springing up.

Someone was whistling a popular music hall tune. The whistler, by the sound, was well aft. Then lazy footfalls coming forward started to accompany the whistling. Jack and Hector pulled themselves along and slipped behind the funnel on the opposite side. The musician rounded the corner of the funnel. Hector tapped the man on the shoulder. When he turned around, Hector knocked him senseless with one blow. Jack caught the man before he fell and gently lowered him to the deck.

"You didn't let him finish his song," Jack whispered.

"I'm not much of a music lover," Hector whispered back.

They pulled out bandannas from their pockets. Jack gagged the man while Hector tied his hands behind his back. Then Hector glided away and went below. Jack slipped down the down the fore-companion.

The *Antoinette* was once a nice vessel, but now she was in a filthy state. Her decks appeared not to have been washed for months. Her brass work was black, and paint peeled from the woodwork. Matches, ashes and fragments of tobacco were strewn about.

"The crew seemed to like many things more than work," Jack said to himself.

A light streamed from the salon, the door being ajar. Jack cautiously peered in. Lake, Guerin and two evil-faced sailors were playing cards, a whiskey bottle between them along with an empty one on the floor. All were muddled with drink.

Jack's hand slid round the door, and removed the key. He waited a long five minutes, his heart beating faster than usual for the first time that night. Then, inch by inch, he closed the door and inserted the key into the lock.

The tensest moment of all came when he gripped the key. There was a crash as one of the men upset a glass, and the click of the lock tongue was unheard. Jack pocketed the key.

He knew that he must act quickly now. If one of the card players wanted to leave the salon, the discovery of the locked door would cause an immediate alarm. A cracked, hoarse voice whined almost in his ear.

"Dan! Curse and burn ye, ye dog? Give me drink, drink, drink! I'm dyin' for drink."

The voice came from the next cabin. Jack dropped on one knee, his eye at the keyhole. In the darkened cabin, Swayne lay amid a heap of tumbled bedclothes. Jack saw that he was too drunk to recognize anyone. He saw, too, a bottle half-filled with rum.

A violent, deep hatred, blood-red and hot, seized Jack. He wanted revenge. Revenge for the scars on his back, revenge for the indescribable pain he suffered, revenge even for Gaskara's murder. It needed to be a quick act, although he would prefer it to be as slow as Swayne had delivered the thirty-nine strokes. One swift plunging movement with his knife, or perhaps his hands around Swayne's scrawny throat, choking the breath out of him. Or perhaps a pillow over his face, pressing down ... harder and harder.

Jack grasped the doorknob. He could hear his own breathing, tense and labored. He slowly pushed the door open. He stepped in and reached the bed. He grasped the handle of his knife.

"Dan! I'm sick and weak now, but I'll tear the throat out of ye, for this. Rum, rum! Dan, I say! Ye dog, ye hound! Ye ..." Swayne yelled out.

There was an angry shout from one of the poker players in the salon next door. Another call from Swayne may cause one of the crew next door to get up to investigate and discover the locked door. At all risks, Swayne must be quieted immediately. Jack filled a pannikin with the spirit, and handed it to Swayne. Swayne gulped the drink down greedily, and sank back in a stupor.

Jack returned to the passage, slowly closing and locking the cabin door behind him, the key also going in his pocket. The next two cabins were in ruins, with masses of splintered wood blocking the passageway. Jack poked his head through a hole in the wall.

This was obviously where his first shot landed. It struck between this deck and the one below, ripping up the floor. Down below, Jack saw walls blackened by fire and smelled the lingering, acrid odor of smoke. In the ruins of the cabin on the lower deck, he saw the remains of guns and powder boxes. He apparently hit the cabin the crew used as an armory. That caused the explosion and fire, and hastened the end of the *Antoinette's* attack.

I couldn't do that on a bet, Jack thought as he smiled. *Beginner's luck.*

Jack returned to the main deck, stopping to pull the two cabin keys out of his pocket and tossing them overboard. Then he climbed the ladder to the deserted bridge. Moving quickly, he rummaged through the bookshelf next to the chart table, and grabbed the nautical almanac and tidal atlas. As he did, he spotted a tin box. His knife easily forced open the cheap look, revealing a leather-bound book inside. Jack picked it up, and flipped through some of the pages. He whistled softly, and returned the book to the box and tucked it under his arm. He left the broken lock on the table as a message to the captain.

He went to the chart table and scooped up the plotter, the sextant, and the divider, wrapping the whole lot in all of the navigation charts. The compass rested in a gimbals cradle. He lifted the instrument and added it to his plunder. He began to feel giddy, as if just pulling a practical joke at school, and had to stifle a giggle. He went back down to the deck carrying his loot, then pitched the lot over the rail except the box. The skies opened again and the rain pounded down.

Hector came up to him with a mallet and a punch. They moved forward on the deck to the anchor chain. Hector quickly found the pin. Click, click, click rang the punch against the pin, the thundering rain drowning out the noise. The pin had rusted in the shackle, and defied Hector for a long time. Finally, Hector nodded to Jack. Jack grabbed the anchor chain as Hector broke the pin.

Jack strained every muscle stopping the chain from rattling across the deck. Hector joined him grasping the chain, and the two walked the chain as noiselessly as possible toward the hawserhole, finally releasing it. There was a dull splash as the end of the chain hit the water and sank. They had set the vessel adrift.

The sea anchor lay nearby in a messy pile. Without a word between them, Jack and Hector unhitched the sea anchor and also sent it over the side.

They rushed to the railing. Hector climbed down the ratline to the launch. Jack undid the ratline, then dropped it into the water. He dove off the deck and climbed into the launch. Casting off, Hector started the electric motor and pointed the launch toward the island.

The weather had been their ally, but now it violently turned against them. A strong easterly wind blew, whipping up the water into whitecaps. The launch bounced and dove on the waves, as though a wild horse trying to buck off Jack and Hector, threatening to capsize. The rain came in sheets. Hector held the bow into the waves as best he could. Jack crouched up front, peering through the storm.

"There!" Jack shouted over the wind. "There's the bay! A few degrees to the starboard!"

Hector changed course. A wave crashed over the launch, almost swamping it. Jack grabbed a bucket and started bailing.

It seemed like hours battling the storm before they finally entered Shrapnel Bay and reached the *Enigma*. Jack seized the painter and scrambled up the ratline, securing the launch.

"Bring the box!" Jack yelled to Hector, then he hurried into the boat's cabin.

He had just lit the lantern when Hector joined him. He put down the box. They looked at each other and laughed as they braced themselves against the bunks as the *Enigma* pitched in the storm.

"The *Antoinette* just had a visitation from two ghosts," Jack said.

"You look quite substantial for somebody from beyond the grave," Hector replied, and punched Jack in the shoulder.

"Why, thank you, sir. Were you successful?" Jack asked.

Hector put on an expression of mock hurt. "You wound me, sir, to the quick!" He reached into his pocket and pulled out a small valve. "It is going to be very difficult to build up a head of steam without this." He stood up, opened the cabin's hatch, and pitched the valve overboard. "Oops! Oh, dear, oh, dear, how careless of me. Besides, much of the coal is now wet."

"From the rain?"

Hector shook his head and hitched up his pants. Jack laughed.

"What's so important about that?" Hector pointed to the box.

"Ah, this! It appears that the *Antoinette's* captain was keeping a duplicate log." Jack lifted the box onto the top bunk, opened it and withdrew the book. "He seems to have written down everything, and I mean everything, that happened, as well as all of what he heard from Vanderlet and the others. They were quite chatty, Swayne in particular after a few drinks, and the captain seems to be quite the eavesdropper. It's all in here, chapter and verse, including Gaskara's murder. It's as good as a confession. I do believe the captain was going to try his hand at a little blackmail."

"My, my, my. I am shocked — shocked. There is no honor among thieves."

"None whatsoever." Jack tapped the book. "This log, however, is an insurance policy for us, and so it will find a new home in my bank vault. I will also send a copy to Inspector Tasker, with my compliments. When the captain, Vanderlet and the others find out it is missing, I think that will dissuade any further contact from them." Jack shrugged. "Who knows? I may end up owning a schnapps importing firm."

"I wonder where the *Antoinette* will end up?" Hector asked. "There is a strong easterly wind."

"I care not, as long as she is away from here."

"Wouldn't you want to be aboard her tomorrow when they find out they're adrift with no charts, no steam power, and no launch?"

"And no compass, and a single mast. It could prove to be very interesting. It will take some time before they are able to return to civilization," Jack said.

"If ever," Hector added grimly.

"If ever," Jack quietly confirmed.

"Nevertheless, despite the nasty weather, we should still stand watch tonight. I'll take the first one. I might as well go up as is, since I'm dripping wet already." Hector started up the companionway.

"When this storm clears," Jack declared, "we tackle the treasure!"

CHAPTER TWENTY

The next day dawned clear, the air swept clean and fresh from the storm. It was early morning, when Jack, standing the night's last watch on the Hoof, scanned the horizon. Nothing was visible at sea. He peered through the glass. Still empty.

Hector approached him with two mugs of steaming tea. He had some rope and a block and tackle slung over his shoulder.

"Any sign of the *Antoinette*?" asked Hector as he handed one mug to Jack.

Jack smiled a thanks as he took the mug then shook his head. "She's not in sight. Frankly, I hope she's bumping up by the walls of the caldera like some forgotten bathtub toy." He blew on his tea then sipped it.

Hector chuckled, and shifted the rope and block and tackle to the ground. "Now, to get down to business. Namely, transferring the treasure from the cave below to the *Enigma*. I've been thinking ..."

"I thought I heard a strange noise."

"I shall display my magnanimous nature and ignore that doltish remark," Jack returned. "I've worked out a scheme on how to accomplish moving the treasure. When you've finished your wet, meet me at Gaskara's hut."

"Hector, can I ask you a question?"

"Yes, of course."

Jack kept gazing out to sea. "When I was being flogged by Swayne, did I beg for mercy?"

"No, you did not."

Jack nodded and sipped his tea. "Thank you. The answer was important to me."

"I understand. Come to the hut when you're ready."

Since the rain lasted most of the night they stood watch, both he and Hector were still dressed only in their trousers. Jack took a deep breath. The sunlight, weak as it was, felt good on his face and chest.

His mind flashed back to the — he really didn't know what to call it: dream, delirium, or perhaps a peek into the afterlife — and the three figures he saw. He understood his mother and father being there, but his uncle? After their bickering relationship, why was he there?

He remembered his old room at the house, and how it hadn't changed. It was almost as if his uncle kept it as a shrine ... or to the hope that Jack would occupy it again someday.

Unpleasant questions forced their way into his mind. Was his anger at his uncle unreasonable? Was it so great that it blocked any and all other feelings toward him? Had his uncle tried to get along with him and Jack rejected it? Had Jack wasted six years of his life, and perhaps the affection of his uncle, in anger?

He felt a wall inside him begin to buckle. He desperately tried to reinforce it, shore it up, not wanting to experience the emotions he knew were roiling on the other side, but the outward pressure simply increased; the wall bulged out. First some cracks spread, then a few chunks dropped out. Finally,

Jack realized it was futile; he couldn't hold the wall together any longer and he had to give it up. The wall collapsed.

"I'm sorry, uncle. Forgive me," Jack whispered.

Tears started to run down his cheeks. He dropped to his knees, then he began to sob.

About half an hour later, Jack made his way to the hut. Three logs, taken from the hut's roof, lay on the ground. Hector was at work at removing another log from the roof.

"I need three more about the same length as those," he said. He looked at Jack. "Are you all right?"

Jack nodded and smiled. "I made peace with a ghost."

Hector nodded back. "Good. Lend me a hand."

They harvested the needed logs from the roof, shuttled them all to the cave entrance and moved the block and tackle down. Jack fetched a pick, shovel and two lanterns from the *Enigma*.

They finally had all their equipment at the ready. Standing in front of the cave entrance, both still shirtless, Jack shouldering the pick and shovel, holding the lanterns, the two reminded him of coal miners at the start of their shift.

"So, what is your little plan?" Jack rested the pick and shovel on the ground.

"We will lash these three logs together, and that will be our bridge over the pit," Hector explained. "After that, we'll proceed to the next stage."

They made and placed their bridge over the chasm, then carried the last three logs to the lead plate marking the portal to the *Satan's* treasure. After they moved the plate, Hector set to work. He roped the logs into a tripod. It took several attempts to accomplish it, then he attached the block and tackle to the rig. Finally he and Jack set it over the opening in the cave floor.

"Now, we simply attach each chest to the rope, then haul it up to this chamber with the block and tackle," said Hector, patting his creation with one hand with pride, "and then transfer it to the *Enigma*."

"What a clever little monkey!" exclaimed Jack.

Hector took a bow in appreciation. Lighting the second lantern, he dropped into the lower chamber, followed by Jack. They went to the first sea chest, each to one end.

"Lift on the count of three," Hector said as he grabbed the handle. "Ready?"

Jack nodded.

"One, two, three!"

They heaved on the chest. The rotten wood split and cracked, spilling the treasure on the cave floor, leaving Jack and Hector holding the remnants of the chest ends in the air. For a second, they didn't move, then Hector hurled the part of the chest he was holding on the ground with an oath.

"Don't you dare laugh!" Hector growled, jabbing his index finger at Jack. "Not even one little, teeny, tiny titter!"

"I wouldn't dream of it, old chap," Jack covered his laugh by dropping the part of the chest he held and coughing at the same time. "Well, as the saying goes, the best laid plans of mice and men oft go astray."

"Give us a piece of cheese," Hector grumbled as he glared at the glittery mess, fists on his hip.

Jack thought for a moment. "Stop pouting. We still can use your ingenious gadget, I think."

"How so?"

"There's a crate covering the carronade. We bring that crate to the upper chamber along with two buckets. Then one of us fills one bucket with the trinkets, and attaches it to the rope. The other hauls up the filled bucket, takes it to the crate and dumps in the load. Meanwhile, whoever is down here is filling up the second bucket. He sends the full bucket up, while the empty one comes down. We keep going in that fashion until the crate is, say, half to two-thirds full, then we both carry the crate down to the *Enigma*. We load the treasure into her hold, bring the empty crate back here, and so forth."

Hector spread his hands wide in approval. "I knew there was a reason I brought you along."

Carting the treasure out of the cave and down to the *Enigma* turned out to be seemingly as hot and hard as mining for coal. They loaded the crate, trudged down the hill, and deposited its contents into one of the boat's holds, then repeated the process. The pair mechanically walked the circuit over and over and over, plodding like pack mules, sweating so much they looked like they had just been swimming, so tired they couldn't talk. It was late afternoon when they put the last load into the *Enigma's* forward hold. The two collapsed on the deck, too exhausted even to celebrate their newfound wealth.

"They never write about that part of treasure finding," groaned Jack.

A refreshing strong breeze swept over them.

"I hate to say this ..." Hector started.

Jack let out a deep sigh. "But you are going to say it anyway."

"I'm afraid so. We need to take advantage of this wind and the full moon tonight."

"Let me make a guess what you are about to say: we need to weigh anchor."

"Bright lad. I always said you are smarter than you looked." Hector slowly got up. "Time to weigh anchor."

Jack also reluctantly climbed to his feet. Despite both sporting healthy tans, he noticed Hector still showed the marks from the hot poker and the bullet graze to the head. Jack still bore the thin, white line from Swayne's knife on his chest, and he felt the tightness from the whip scars covering his back.

"You seem reflective," Hector observed.

"I was just thinking what a strange journey we have been on, my friend," Jack said.

"It has been quite an adventure, my brother. I thank you for permitting me to join you on it." Hector stuck out his hand, and Jack firmly shook it. "Now weigh that anchor and stand by the sails."

Jack saluted and smiled. "Aye-aye, sir."

They hauled in the anchor. Jack went to man the sails, while Hector took charge of the tiller.

The sails caught the wind. The *Enigma* responded smartly to the tiller, left Shrapnel Bay and headed into open waters. Jack stood in the stern, watching Peril Island slowly recede behind them in the gathering dusk.

Jack watched a curious plume rise from the volcano's peak. It was not a flame, but the reflection of fire on a gush of steam, such as is seen when the furnace door of a locomotive is open at night. Presently jagged forks of red danced in and out among it. Reports boomed from the volcano in swift succession. Then, all at once, a glowing crimson pillar rose skyward, bringing the island into vivid view. It lasted perhaps a second or more.

"Old Nick seems to be stirring up his big pot," Jack noted. "You were right about Peril Island. It may not be around much longer."

Jack watched the eruption for a few minutes.

"This whole experience seems so unreal," he said, "like it was something you read in the Sunday supplements."

"You go ahead and write about it. Put me down for a copy," said Hector.

Jack laughed. "Who would believe it?"

"Well, it really did happen to us. We both have the scars to prove it," replied Hector. "Perhaps you should save it as a bedtime story for your children."

"Perhaps. I'll scare them to sleep," Jack said.

A bright light — a flare — suddenly appeared in the sky over the eastern end of the island behind the volcano. It burned for a few minutes as it dropped out of sight behind the mountains.

"Hector! That was a ship's distress rocket!" Jack exclaimed.

"Nonsense," Hector replied flatly. "It was the volcano."

"No, no, I'm positive it was a distress signal. We need to —" Jack stopped. There was only one other ship in the area, and he knew who was on it. He knew what they did to him, what they did to Hector, what they did to Gaskara. Vanderlet could be using the distress rocket as a lure, to set a trap, trusting in Jack's basic decency. In this case, Vanderlet was wrong. Jack turned his back to Peril Island. "I guess you're right. It was just the volcano."

The *Enigma* seemed to know that she was heading back to her home port, and fairly flew over the water despite her heavy cargo. A few days of easy sailing later, Jack and Hector sat on the deck, basking in the warmth of the sun. The sea was calm, and the tiller tied down to the correct course. Jack labored over a notebook while Hector read.

"Phew!" Jack breathed out as he put down his pencil. "This is more complicated than I had imagined. Look at this list! One, get the treasure to London, without every footpad in the country learning about it. Two, secure treasure in vault. Three, sort treasure into types. Four, determine which pieces should be donated to museums. Five, sell the rest. Six, hire a solicitor, although I'll probably use Mr. Halliday and the accountancy firm I already have. Seven, form a charity board of directors. By the way, I've put you on the board."

"Delighted, of course."

"Eight, determine how and to whom to donate money. Those are just the broad strokes. The devil is in the details." Jack put the notebook down. "I can't believe I haven't asked you yet. What are you going to do with your half of the treasure?"

"I was rather thinking about giving much of it to you and Agnes as a wedding present," Hector glanced up at Jack. "Why, you're blushing, old chap."

"All right, Hector, for once and for all," Jack leaned forward, tapping the deck for emphasis. "Who are you?"

Hector didn't look up from his book. "I already told you once."

"You never!" Jack protested.

"I did."

"When?" Jack demanded.

"The first night in front of your house, while we stood on the stoop," Hector replied as if it were the most obvious thing in the world.

"As if I haven't had enough puzzles already during this affair. The first night in front of my house ..." Jack mumbled. He closed his eyes, trying to recall the conversation. "Ah, let me see ... you were being obstinate, and then I think I said something along the lines that for all I know you could a lost prince or lord or somebody."

"A baronet," Hector corrected.

"Oh, pull the other one ..." Jack snapped. He stopped as he realized what Hector meant. "Wait, wait. Are you truly telling me you are —"

Hector nodded. "The eighth baronet of Mansford."

For a full minute, the only sound came from the slap of the ocean against the *Enigma's* hull and the snap of her sails. Jack sputtered something incoherent.

"Or, more to the point, I will be," Hector closed his book, placed it next to him on the deck, and folded his hands in his lap. "I will assume the title upon the death of my father, which I pray will not be for many, many years yet. At that time, I will also inherit Dane House in the city, Dane Abbey and the surrounding farmlands in the country, plus something like eighty thousand a year income. It is possible that my father, who has a bit of a miserly streak, may have hoarded up a vast more amount of money more by that time. Do close your mouth, Jack. You look like a codfish."

"But ... but, you are as rich as Croesus, and you were shoveling coal!" Jack stammered out.

"You are not the only youth to leave home, although mine was happily under different circumstances," Hector said. "Your parents died when you were young, and then you had, shall we say, a tumultuous relationship with your guardian uncle, which finally pushed you to hook it. I, on the other hand, have a good relationship with my parents. I accompanied them to weekends at country estates, polo matches at Hurlingham, sailing —"

"That is why you knew all about sailing the *Enigma*, from sailing yachts!" Jack exclaimed. "You never worked on her when she was a fishing boat."

"No," Hector held up his hand. "No, that was true. I did work on the *Enigma*, and the captain did get sick. I've held a Board of Trade certificate since I was fifteen."

"Of course you have."

Hector laughed. "Jealous. I was taken on the crew because I knew about sailing. I didn't learn about sailing from working on the *Enigma*. Although, I must admit, my father helped me meet the boat's purchase price."

"I still don't understand why you left your parents."

"It may be difficult to explain to someone who hasn't experienced a certain kind of life. My upbringing was loving, but it was constricted ... very controlled. I attended the proper schools, the correct events, learned which piece of silverware to use for which meal course. Unfortunately, it was to me a very narrow world. Dull, in point of fact. I did not want to end up a knut, going to party after party just to fill up my idle time. So I negotiated a release, as it were. My parents agreed, not readily, not happily, but they finally agreed, with conditions which I have followed. I keep in regular contact with them. When we were in port and I couldn't get off the ship because we were coaling, those letters I asked you to post were to them. I also visit frequently. In fact, I had just completed one when I met you on the dock." He noted Jack's expression. "You don't seem to believe me."

"I ... I don't know if I do or not," Jack floundered.

"Simple enough matter to prove. We shall pay a visit to my parents upon our return. I've told them about you, and they'd like to meet you." Hector pointed to the scar which started over his left eye. "We may have to change portions of our story for my mother's benefit. She's quite the worrier."

"Why didn't you tell me sooner? Didn't you trust me?"

Hector shook his head. "No, it had nothing to do with not trusting you. I was afraid of you."

"You? Afraid? Afraid of me?"

Hector sighed. "I know that, eventually, I will have to return to my parents' world when I assume the title. To quote your uncle, it is my duty. I was afraid if you knew who I really was, where I truly came from, it would fracture our friendship. I was afraid that you would be insulted. That you would think I was just some upper-class twit, descending from the grand manor house to see how the common folk lived or that I was just slumming, and all that."

He was pensive for a moment. "I have many acquaintances in that other world, but no real friends. Oh, there are the young bloods who think of the big shoots and tasty dinners at Dane Abbey, and the fading aristocrats with marriageable daughters who recollect that Hector Dane is the catch of the season. It's flies after the honey, old chap. When I have to return to that world, at least I hope to retain my only true friend, my only brother, I have ever had."

Jack didn't say anything for a moment. He stood, and faced Hector.

"You need not worry. Of course, your social class has no effect on our friendship. And now," he bowed with extreme formality, and intoned with over-precise, snooty correctness, "Sir Hector Dane, eighth baronet of Mansford, hop to it and empty the slop bucket."

Jack ducked the thrown book.

Made in United States
Orlando, FL
30 October 2023

38406870R00124